Playing for the Game

BHUPENDRA SINGH

notionpress.com

INDIA · SINGAPORE · MALAYSIA

ISBN 979-8-88749-320-6

Contents

Introduction

Golf is a ball-and-club sport. A few centuries ago, it began as a commoner's sport on the coastal sands of Scotland but quickly gripped the fascination of the rich and royals of those times. Eventually, it acquired the patronage of the nobility and with time it thrived. Though the Scottish seaside links with their rolling greens served as a cradle for the game, presently it is an international sport played popularly across the globe by more than 60 million golfers. Golf is a unique sport invented by mankind. It is different from all other sports because no other sport imitates the philosophy of life as closely as golf does, in its entirety!

A long time back when I had a chance introduction to the game, it was its philosophical aspect that fascinated me the most. When I explored the game further, I realized that it mimics human life in an interesting manner. I then thought of telling the story of the game and its subtle similarities with life to those who were still oblivious of the game.

I, therefore, had decided to write a story about golf a long time back but weaving words was a challenge for a first-time fiction writer. Nonetheless, after a continued striving, eventually I succeeded in knitting a story about the game and am pleased to bring it to the readers.

In the following chapters, I have attempted to introduce the game and its philosophy. I trust anyone who is inclined to sports or philosophy or for that matter the nature of life, would find some sort of connect with the game and its story. I am sure the readers will get a glimpse of the golfing world through this piece of work which otherwise remains exclusive to a few fortunate ones. If you are not a golfer, the story would introduce the game of golf to you, and if you are a golfer already the game would reintroduce itself to you as you turn the pages.

In the following paragraphs, I am introducing the basic terminology and technical aspects of the game for the benefit of readers who are not golfers. It would help them grasp the game and the story better. If you are already a golfer and understand the golfing lingo you may skip the following section and switch to the Prologue directly.

In the game of golf, a player plays a golf ball using various kinds of clubs. In golf parlance, the term 'club' is used in two contexts; one, the sticks (equipment) which are used to hit the balls and the other to refer to a group (of golfers who come together to play golf), and so the place where they come to play golf is also called a 'golf club'.

A golf course actually is a long pitch of sprawling grass on which the game is played, generally as a round of eighteen holes. It is often a stretch of about 7000 yards or more in distance which is divided into eighteen segments or holes. The game is played from a starting hole to a finishing eighteenth hole, in a set order, one after the other to complete a round of golf.

Unlike pitches for other sports, the golf course, however, is a vast area of acres of turfgrass cover. It is often set amidst a natural ambience merging intricately with the local landscape which serves as a fitting pitch for a grand game. This kind of flexible pitch premise gives golfers an opportunity to play the game in a variety of natural topographies.

As there are no set pitch size standards or rigid specifications for a golf course layout to be a golf course, every golf course in the world is unique in its design and setting. Golf course architects while crafting courses use their creativity freely to suit the local landscapes and make their courses mimic 'nature in miniature'. Nature, however, remains the master architect, dictating largely the character of any golf course.

Consequently, the overall game becomes a kind of a walk through nature where a golfer keeps striking his golf ball from a starting area called 'teeing ground' till he reaches a target area called 'putting green' of a hole. He eventually sinks the ball into a hole that is cut into the putting green and identified by a pole with a flag. A player plays holes one after the other completing a loop of eighteen holes that makes a round in golf.

Again, the term 'hole' is used in two different contexts in golf; one as a unit or segment of a course consisting of a 'teeing area', a 'putting green', and a distance (about 250 yards to 550 yards or more) in between the two, while the other is a hole (four-inch and a quarter in diameter) in the putting green per se.

Golf courses may have different cuts of grass height resulting in different kinds of ball lies which consequently calls for a variety of strokes and club choices starting from the tee, but the grass on the putting green is usually cut to a short height to make it a surface suited for rolling a golf ball. A ball on a green is generally played with a stroke intended to roll it into the hole, thus the stroke is called 'putt' which is made with a specific club called 'putter' and that specific area of the course a 'putting green'.

In between the tee and green, there are other areas too which are known differently in golf parlance. The 'fairway' is one such area which usually is in the middle and is fairly well prepared and so players preferably try to land their golf balls in it while progressing toward the green. 'Rough' is an adjoining area usually on either side of the fairway, where the grass and vegetation are rough and wild. A player, therefore, tries to avoid such areas because making the next stroke from such an area is a relatively difficult task.

To add to the difficulty for players, in between the tee and green there may be pits consisting of sand. These are called 'bunkers' and because playing a ball from sand is difficult, players try to avoid such sand traps too. Further, a challenge may be encountered by the players in the form of water bodies in a course like lakes, ponds, rivers or creeks. These may be natural or man-made in a golf course and are called 'penalty areas'. There could be other defined penalty areas too in a course, from where if a player wants to get off, he has to add a penalty stroke to his score or play the ball as it lies.

However, to deal with the challenges of the game, sometimes a player also has help in the form of a 'caddie' who is any person accompanying a player on the course and assisting him in his game by carrying a bag of clubs for him. A caddie is also authorized to advise him in playing different shots when asked for.

A player keeps his score on a card called 'scorecard' which he submits to the committee in charge of the course called 'green committee' after finishing a round. The committee is responsible for deciding the result of a round or competition and declaring the results.

Though golf is played in different formats and originally it evolved as a 'match-play', but the 'stroke-play' format is a popular one in professional competitions in present times where a player who plays a round in a minimum number of strokes turns out to be a winner for that round. Also, in club golf, players generally move and play in groups of four, each playing his golf ball, thereby the group itself is referred to as 'fourball'.

The other interesting concept is 'par' in golf; each of the 18 holes in a golf course is of different lengths and designs that are designated a par rating according to the adjudged difficulty level. A par 3 hole is the shortest in golf, where a golfer is expected to reach the green in 1 stroke and then put the ball into the hole with two more strokes by rolling it on the green. Similarly, a par 4 hole is longer and requires 2 strokes to reach the green and 2 putting strokes, and par 5 is still longer where 3 strokes are expected from a golfer to reach the green with two strokes to putt on the green to finish the hole. Though 2 strokes are considered for putting on the green, the player may do so in a more or lesser number of putting strokes based on his skills.

With par, comes up other scoring terms in golf like 'birdie' and 'bogey'. If a player plays a hole in strokes as is represented by the par rating of a hole, it is said to be played par, if he finishes the hole in 1 stroke less, it is called a birdie score. If a hole is finished in 2 strokes less than the designated par, it is called an 'eagle' in golfing lingo. Similarly, if a golfer takes 1 extra stroke to finish a hole it is called a 'bogey', 2 extra strokes a 'double bogey' and so on.

During professional golf tournaments, the players' scores are often presented on boards called 'leaderboards' for spectators and the players. For distinction and easy reading, the score is generally written in red colour if the score is under par, in blue if it is over par, and the par score for a hole is represented in black colour.

The game is played with discipline and is governed by a set of complex rules. Also, the 'rule book' is followed religiously in the game, word to word without default. The game may appear confusingly intricate, for sure it is mysteriously melodramatic. However, if one gathers the guts to get on to the course and begins to play it in the spirit of the game, golf also turns out to be the simplest game, it unfolds itself with every stroke, just like life!

Prologue: The Game

Joy stretched his golf club for a backswing, but he froze for a few moments in the same posture on seeing a bee. A very unlucky bee was hovering over a bright bloom on the stalk of which a mantis was clinging. Camouflaged completely, the mantis in its innocent praying posture patiently waited for the moment, with absolute stillness. The bee, oblivious of the mantis and its hunger, came close, a little more close, and then there was a flick of forelimbs; the bee was there in the claws of the mantis.

The spectacle that unfolded on a branch of a tree at the foot of which Joy's golf ball lay in a difficult lie, was violently rhapsodic. The game of life concluded in front of him, after a brief pause, perhaps picking winning cues from nature he continued with his own game. He skilfully extricated his ball from the thicket that ran all along the fairway of the golf course that he was playing. From the rough stuff of the forest where he stood trapped a few moments ago, he was again back on the fine fairway turf.

The virtues of patience and perseverance with which Joy continued his strike in the game were becoming a champion. He was a true seeker of the game; he was focused, he was precise, and he was passionate. He never gave in under the pressures of the game. Even during the most daunting moments of the sport, he stood steadily without a waver, always. Joy's calm disposition often helped him walk out of such rough situations without much scathing on his scorecard. His precision skill of swinging a club at a golf ball even in the most difficult of lies matched that of the performance of the mantis on the bee.

It is true that in larger games of life winning is the other name for survival. Therefore, most games on the turf are competitive and are played for survival where winning is the only object for a player in the field. In such games, victory or at least a hope of victory is the sole motivator for a player to keep playing and remain in the game.

Joy too must have had his own motivations, but someday with his great playing skills whether he would emerge as a real champion or not, only time will tell. In a golf course, regardless of the players and their potential to perform, the game never stops, irrespective of how it concludes!

Playing is a natural instinct with which we are born, and when a play gets structured with regulations it becomes a game. All games are guided by rules, and golf is no exception, it has its own code that governs it. The rule book of the game may appear long and lengthy but interestingly many golfers spend their entire lives playing golf without flipping even the first few pages of the rule book and that too without a falter.

It is natural to have a curiosity that how a golfer is able to play the game without knowing all the rules. It is so because as long as a golfer is honest in his acts and is fair to his fellow players he is good to go with his game even without reading the rule book in its entirety. In the game, as long as a player does what he does with a right intent and does what is fair to the field, he is on a right track. In one word, 'intent' is the premise within which all regulations of the game are written.

Therefore, despite all its complexities, a true seeker and a genuine practitioner of the game never gets it wrong. It comes naturally to its players, the game is easy, and a player just has to go with it rather than against it. Probably it was intended to be such, and it is the sheer simplicity of the game that it has been played and appreciated the world over by the kings and commons alike, for ages. It has remained so even to this date; one has to just drain a small ball in a hole, of course, following fair ways!

The guiding principle of the game has been simpler, 'play the ball as it lies, and play the course as you find it'. Period. It is the core principle on which the great game was founded and it is still thriving on this very rock foundation. It is a game of skills, focus, precision, passion, and hard work, but also of possibilities, probabilities, miracles, luck, and hope.

The beauty of the game lies in the fact that it is the only sport where a player referees himself in his game. He is expected to play fair even if nobody is watching, and interestingly the traditions of the sport are honoured and expectations are mostly met. In case of an inadvertent breach of a rule, it is the responsibility of a player to apply penalties to himself, and when in doubt seek help from the keepers of the code.

The game has been continuing since perpetuity and it is bound to thrive till eternity. And, when the players who play it prove their greatness time and again, why it wouldn't. The gentlemen golfers guard it with their own honour by staying true to themselves and by playing it in the spirit of the game. True, in the spirit of the game lies its beauty. But sometimes we wonder, if it is the greatness of the game or that of its players that makes it beautiful. The players seem to carry an insatiable curiosity and urge about the game, the more they explore, the more they want to play it.

Though, in the field, every player plays his own unique game, the game however has essentially remained the same since the very beginning. The governing tenet for the rules has been the same since perpetuity. The game has been played repeatedly by many players, time and again, prior to the present players on the same field and will also be played after them, yet each player sees it differently and plays the same game differently. The mysterious game is all about perspective. It is the intent of the player with which one plays that makes it different, for 'intent' is at its core.

For some it is just a struggle, for others, it's an opportunity to perform and win while for some others it is just a stroll of pleasure from a tee to a green. Some see it as a game of luck, for some, it is a pure skill while others see it as a mix of both. Whatever it may be, it is interesting to remain in the game irrespective of one's perspective and the outcome of the game at the end. Winning and losing is part of the game, so it is expected that one never quits it for fear of losing, if one is granted with an honour to be there on the turf, it should be honoured duly.

In the game, a player always has an opportunity to choose what is right for him and get back to the fairway even if he lands in a rough for any reason. He is free to choose his club, if not the lie of the ball. He is free to choose a stroke, if not the result of that stroke. A player in the game is endowed with a choice of free will. Since the game has granted the power of choice to its players, in all fairness every player is expected to owe the responsibility of a stroke that he chooses to make irrespective of the outcome that it leads to.

The outcome of a stroke is not in the hands of players, but no action goes without an outcome. This makes the game interesting; everyone is free to speculate but none knows it with certainty. The results are deemed certain only when they are posted on the board of time. The true teller of the results is always time; an ultimate referee, and a supreme jury.

Interestingly, although a player has a choice of making a stroke of his liking, and he always attempts to drive his golf ball in the intended direction, he has no control over the ball once it leaves the face of his club after a stroke.

The lie, in which his ball will eventually land is not in his control. Sometimes even the best-executed shots with the best judgment can get a 'rub of the green'. The finely struck shots may accidentally hit unintended objects and land in undesirable areas in unfavourable lies. After all, we don't exist in isolation, we are influenced by our surroundings and we too contribute to the larger cosmic game, howsoever small our strokes may be.

A 'rub of the green' is sheer luck, true. So, it is natural that a player is pleased if it is in his favour but cringes if it places him in a tough lie, he also gets envious if it helps a fellow competitor and tends to complain about it, cursing the game for being unfair. However, the advantages and disadvantages that result from a shot are on an individual basis but if one has an eye to see the round holistically from a larger perspective, one would realize that everything gets evened out in the long run. With experience, we realize that the luck in the game just makes it interesting. The real enlightened ones in a competition, therefore conduct themselves without being too happy when luck favours them and being too sad when it works against them.

The players of the game are known for their indomitable spirit and fair approach in dealing with the golf course even when they find themselves in an ugly stretch while they are in the field. Eventually, hope is the rope that swings players of the game through all the good, bad, and ugly stretches of the adventurous track.

Sometimes we get good breaks and some other times bad ones, but as long as one is hopeful and is striking the ball, every player in the field is a potential champion. Like a gentleman, with honour, any ordinary player can transcend to an extraordinary level of sportsmanship while consistently treading on the track. The game is not only about playing for a trophy but it is worth playing for honour too.

Some people prefer to play for a purpose, and they keep looking for one in the game. However, what other purpose one would wish for, if he is blessed with a beautiful partner and has begun to cherish the play itself; some players play it for the sheer joy of playing.

By the time Joy found his way back on the fairway, Jasmine, his playing partner and childhood friend had already reached the green. Her ball lay a few feet from the pin but she waited for Joy to reach the green before making her next putting shot. Joy made a perfect pitch shot from the fairway, and his ball taking a low loft landed safely on the green next to where Jas' was lying. He then continued silently on his short walk to the green, probably reflecting about the deftness of the stroke executed by the mantis or maybe pitying the fate of the bee.

Joy and Jas were amateur golfers, a very promising one indeed! Joy had been shining on the men's amateur circuit and Jas had been a recent sensation on the women's amateur golf circuit in the country. They restricted themselves to the zone of amateur golf because they planned to finish their college first, before getting into the grind of professional golf. Also, before entering the big club of competitive golf, the college has offered them an opportunity to stay close to each other, a little more, be it under the pretext of finishing their studies.

They were on a weeklong vacation from their university. They flew all the way back from the Scottish town known for its oldest university and golf courses to the capital city of their own country so as to participate in the 'National Open Amateur Championship'. The tournament was due to be held on the weekend.

Joy was confident that before they fly back to the UK to continue with their university studies, he would have the Amateur Championship in his name. Because his biggest motivator and friend, Jas had accompanied him this time too, she was there by his side to see him win the championship. Playing and practising golf with Jas, his best mate before entering any competition made him happy, confident, and composed.

When we look for a story in a game, it essentially turns out to be a story of its players. A trail of emotions that begins with the birth of a player. However, once born such stories continue to be told and retold for eternity, even after the players who played the game are gone. Golf too is a full circle of emotions and every player in it is a story in itself with moments of joy, struggle, and pain. Aspirations and hope.

The world is replete with stories about the game and its players and if we reflect a little, we realize that all games are games within a game. In life, we play many games, and sometimes life itself appears to be a game. Is, a life different than a game? However, the story of Jas and Joy was born at a golf course of a capital city; the course where they found each other and played their best game ever.

PART 1

The Course

The capital city existed since the very beginning; it was there even before the boundaries of the nation got solidified. The city had always been the centre of power, an abode of art, and a fountainhead of fashion, music, and literature for a vast country.

The capital was a city of dreams, a display of evolving culture, and a seat of changing regimes, but it was never the same. The city being a seat of power had witnessed a continued struggle between the old and the new; one regime replacing the other. Every dynasty that dominated it and every ruler that ruled added or altered the fabric of the ancient city.

As they left one after the other, they also left their indelible marks on the sheets of history. A little dig in the layers of time often brings the buried past of the capital to the fore. The rich remains of the past exist even today and can be seen scattered all over the capital.

Though the city was shaped and reshaped steadily with time, the art and artificiality of the capital in its modern form were set in cement about a century ago when the magical powder from Portland began to cast its spell. Since then, structures of varied shapes began to dot the landscape of capital in concrete, giving it its modern landmarks.

Architecture is lasting memorabilia of an era gone by, it also reflects the social frame of the people who lived and left. The capital demonstrates the old era and a new age vividly in its two towns; the Old and the New.

Within the ruined walls of the old city, the old era still appears animated, having its own unique character and legacy. The charm of the past era is obvious in the art and anatomy of the old city. It has a network of narrow streets and tight lanes, leading to weird endings and quirky quarters.

On the other side, the modern aspirations of the country and that of the residents of the capital in particular, are typically reflected in the new town that grew around the old core with its saucy streets and airy architecture. Wide-open roads circling big roundabouts, bifurcating into perpendiculars, and neatly splitting residential sectors into blocks stated the free-thinking and open mindset of a new generation. The geometrically crafted structures and uniformly chalked-out streets of the city that follow mathematical symmetry and civic functionality appear to have come pixel to pixel on the ground from a decided blueprint of the capital city.

However, in this spree of modernization, the ever-hungry monster of mortar nibbled away almost all green patches of the city, and the cancerous clout of concrete and glass gripped the capital to its core. Ever-expanding complexes of bricks and blocks kept cropping up in every corner of the street. The skyscrapers of the city kept soaring as if on pursuit of piercing the sky.

The human ambition to keep casting intangible ideas into reality with the aid of modern materials continued. Eventually, it led to the paving of every path and passage of the capital in stone, but somehow in the centre of the city, a golfing shrine survived. The golf course warded off the concrete cacodemon from spreading its tentacles in its premises. It fought all attempts of encroachments and surprisingly succeeded in all of them as if the god of golf descended himself onto the grounds to keep the sacred land of the game intact.

The golf course survived! It survived in its sombre beauty and its greens grew and flourished. Slowly, with time, the course began to command respect as the holy land of golf amongst the seekers of the game in the country. Its fame and glory spread far and wide and it became an ultimate pilgrimage for golfers across the country.

Every golfer in the country began to nurture a wish to walk its grounds, at least once in their lifetime. Its pure green turf stretched from the foot of its clubhouse to as far as an eye could see. The grounds matted with grassy velvet became the biggest asset of the capital and the golf course began to state its presence standing high and mighty in its classical character. The course is now the only breathing spot of natural greens in the city, therefore some call it 'Lungs of the City', others call it 'Capital Golf Club', and for some others, it is just 'CGC'.

No two golf courses in the world are the same, they differ, and so are not comparable! The Capital Golf Club too has its own class, character, and charm. Nestled in the centre of the capital, it is a unique course. The course is an old natural beauty in its living form that is still there to bless the residents of the capital. It is believed to have been born with the capital city itself and is considered as ancient as the capital.

More than a century ago, when a new plan for a new town of the capital was drawn, a provision for a new parliament building and a president's palace was made, and to fit the foreign architect's fancy or the layout of the new capital city, acres of forests were felled. The spree continued unabated at a frightening rate till some laws were passed to prevent any further felling of trees in the capital by the parliament. But the laws came a little too late, now one can take any radial route from the centre of the city and drive for miles, for hours, rarely encountering any sizable clump of trees or a natural grove.

However, trees do thrive in the heart of the capital in the premises of CGC, not to the boundless extent as they existed once but as a specimen forest enclosed within the boundary walls. The walls prevent a free walk-in, ensuring the preservation of whatever is left. Although there are two gates of entry to the golf course, not all have an entry pass. Moreover, its entrance matches nowhere the magnificence to which they lead, so most people never bother to get in. The gates of CGC are inconspicuous and are camouflaged with a weather-beaten boundary wall that is mostly shrouded with tree overhangs and heaps of moss and creepers that grow all over it. Within those walls, however, exists a treasure of trees and ancient flora that blooms in its full glory right in the heart of the capital.

No one can hide a two-hundred acre of green beauty in a vault, it is there, sprawling all in open. But still, most people fail to notice it. They pass by it every morning while driving all the way to their work offices on the roads that run along its boundary. Still, they miss it, for their eyes are not on the ground but on the skyscrapers. On their daily chase for money, they are always in a hurry to reach somewhere; a routine rut, an unending pursuit.

At CGC, the greens roll gently. They meander and make their way gracefully winding and unwinding through the thicket. The woods through which these greens flow dramatically are untouched even today. Under the strict guard of golfing knights at CGC the chaste charm of the thriving forest is wholly conserved.

The forest is ancient, it predates not only the golf course but probably the game itself. After all, the trees were the first natives of the land, though later on, a contest for domination was restricted amongst the citizens of the capital themselves. But even today, the botanists, silviculturists, and researchers who visit this virgin land to study ecology and environment often agree that the forest of CGC is a natural lab, existing in its original form. It is now a treasure worth preserving for future generations.

While chasing their golf balls, golfers are the frequent visitors to these forests, especially the beginners. Those who are new in the game and to the course, land in the forest very often. Their golf balls usually leave the wide velvety turf and drift to the doors of the forest. In golf, driving a ball straight is a challenge in itself.

Whether golfers like it or not, to retrieve the golf balls they have to walk to the wild and deal with the jungle on a daily basis, but how the forest treats its trespassers largely depends on the season of the year. It is thin and airy in summers but thick and rampant during rains.

To golfers, the forest is usually more forgiving during the dry season. In summers, when a golf ball gets into its woody hiding, golfers find it easier to seek their golf ball from a thin and dry forest. A little help from caddies in search and a little turning of leafy litter with the Irons is enough for a player to retrieve his ball from the forest floor without much of a hassle.

But, as the forest gets drenched with the first showers of the season, entering forest lines is a given risk, sometimes, even considered foolish. Therefore, every sane player avoids over adventure during rains, a golfer quickly gives up to avoid any entangle with the forest, and the ball is considered lost once it is on its woody trail.

Water is a life sap for a forest, with a touch of rain it assumes activity quickly. Young trees and the young branches on the old trees acquire a flush overnight. Immediately after the rains, with new sprouts growing all over, the forest gets creative with its colourful art. For a few days, its canopy becomes a canvas that displays dabs of red and purple; the colour of fresh flushes of new leaves in their varying stages of growth. In the next few days, the intermittent colour streaks merge into one; everything gets painted in the only colour of nature, the green, and its shades.

Eventually, the transformation is complete and a thin, tan-brown forest of summer becomes a thick, dense ethereal green of a rainy season. Brown trunks of trees gather green moss going all green, rising creepers crawl all around their girth and make them even greener. The growing vines hurriedly ascend to the treetops, their tendrils dangle left and right as if looking for a prop to twine and rise to the sky. They appear to be on a mission as if determined to dig deep into the blue.

The spectacle of CGC during rains is indescribable. After rains, not only forests but the life energy is so eclectic and intense that no area and no soul is left untouched from its effect. Such that, the scrolls of vines hang, twist, and curl all over the eaves and rafters of the clubhouse. The frills of creepers ascend up and spread all over as if on a search of someone. They appear to reach the golfers' door as if to call them, coaxing them to come out in open where the nature is in its playful mood. Golfers' spirits too are forged in steel which neither bends nor dampens in a drizzle. Golfers are not scared of any ground howsoever slippery it may be. The rains rather challenge them, and many of them are seen trudging the tracks like a warrior till they finish, proving their mettle, all wet and drenched.

In the rainy season, CGC is not only a treat to the eyes but also music to the ears; receiving cues from the sky the sorceress nature comes up with her orchestra. In the course, during the daytime birdies fly all over, in the wild and on the greens. After feasting heartily on a mouthful of worms they play tunes of various tones. The chirrups reverberate through the forest silenced only occasionally by a stray ball that may land deep into the forest ricocheting against the towers of trees with a thundering crash.

The night is reigned by insects who take centre stage, singing in their nocturnal chorus. The forest choir issues notes which may range from music to din depending on the mood of the listener. However, whatever it is, it reaches its crescendo intermittently without a trace of its performers, though the darkness is burnt in bits every now and then with flying flickers; the little lamps of nature, the glow-worms.

As the day breaks in, the course is again a verdant beauty. However, what a course is, if there is no game! Steadily, the beauty gets wilder, and the game of woods gets intense; an insect traps a fly, a frog hunts the insect, which in turn becomes a game for a sneaky snake. Occasionally, snakes sneak out even to the golfer's turf, but golfers fear nothing. Handling hazards of the game is their routine affair. The risk is worth the beauty of the course and the fun in the game.

The game is fun but equally, it is about focus and serious concentration. At CGC, however, the distractions are many; a brood of young coots may cross the path of golfers and they will have to respect their right of way. As one is about to swing for his perfect shot, in a jiffy, a herd of deer may cross the fairway. A golfer preparing to putt with his head down, eyes on a golf ball, concentrating to map an intended roll of the ball on a green with a broken contour, may miss a foot-long putt with a sudden chirrup of a cuckoo.

But for this, can nature be blamed? Isn't a golfer's game, an interruption to the games of nature? As long as we respect each other, all games can coexist; nature is generously fair to everybody. Also, true players play against all odds with grace and gratitude.

If played with a sportsman spirit, a round of golf is an organic experience, an opportunity to connect with nature, self, and possibly with the creator of all this charm; the source of all magic around us. It teaches us how to keep moving and keep striking the ball for the pure joy of playing irrespective of how many birdies one makes or how many putts get missed. The game makes one patient and a round of golf turns out to be a humbling experience. For a golfer, it is an opportunity to break off from the vicious circle of daily monotony, to pull out a few hours of relaxation from the race, and at times an opportunity to reflect on the very race that is being run outside the boundary of a golf course.

Not only in CGC but in any golf course, a round of golf is no less than a quick walk of an entire life; a recap of all that has passed and a rapid rundown of all that one could expect in his future. In a golf course, even if someone is a mere spectator, he could still have a joyful time just by keeping his eyes open and silently observing the players, their game, and the endless turf.

With white lilies and pink lotuses blooming all around in the blue of a lake, it is an ethereal stage to see a grand game in action. It is equally impressive a turf for the culmination of such a glorious game. To watch golfers picking golf balls from the pocket of the earth at the 18th green is a pure joy in itself, where they flag in with a finishing feel on their faces. Not everyone is a winner in a game but it is a game worth playing for the sake of the spirit of the game!

Also, a round of golf necessarily doesn't have to end at the 18th. At times, a player's bonding with the course and his playing peers could continue to linger to the bar. In the kingdom of golf, a clubhouse is considered the 19th hole, where every player is rewarded irrespective of his score which he signs for before walking into the house. In the clubhouse, everyone is comforted with the warmth of the fireplace, and a sip from a goblet raises the spirits. It is a perfect culmination for a larger-than-life experience, called golf.

However, to the lesser mortals to whom the game has not yet revealed itself, or unfortunately they have failed to discover the game and its greatness, life remains merely a routine rut of wealth creation.

Players played golf in CGC, but outside its boundary people pursued money. The world beyond the boundary of the club continued to be all about business and wealth. Skyscrapers kept soaring to their vertical limits and streets got stuffed to their capacity. This, however, made CGC one of the most coveted and premium realties on the planet.

Many marketers and business brokers tried to breach the walls of CGC. They tried to encroach its turf on the pretext of creating wealth at a premium for the club. But all these years, the club kept its calm and grew its grass in silence.

The Club

The golf course in the capital existed for a long but even before the course found its ground it was the club that was founded in the capital. In those days, a few friends who had few more friends of Scottish roots, and who shared a common passion for playing the game of golf got together to form a club, the Capital Golf Club. However, initially, there were not many takers for a foreign game of ball and sticks, and the club existed as a small social group where families of a few influentials of the city came together to spend their leisure time amongst the equals, in private.

In the formative years of the club, not many golfers were there in the capital to appreciate the beauty of the game, only a few people who had Scottish roots or those who were in their circle played the game. In the beginning, there were not many patrons for the golf course too, and especially during the times of war, the club and the course struggled even for its very existence.

However, things have changed quickly in the past few decades. It was not only the price of the club's realty that was appreciated but the appreciation for the game also has grown immensely among the citizens of the capital. The applications seeking membership for the club have shot up steeply in the recent past.

One would wonder, whether it was the magnetism of the game that began to bewitch people or it was the outcome of a capitalistic boom that corrupted people, making them play with their *nouveau riche*. Or it has something to do with the 'Tiger Woods' phenomenon' which had gripped the fancy of the world in the decade gone by. Whatever the cause may be, mysteriously from the thin air of the capital, with every passing year more and more golfers came probing for the greens to putt.

The certain spurt in the affinity for greens amongst the citizens of the capital made CGC the busiest golf course on the planet. Initially, newcomers were welcomed, and whosoever was willing to pay a hefty fee, membership was granted. But when the club reached its carrying capacity, no more admittance was possible.

Consequently, some bylaws of the club constitution were amended and a ceiling was imposed. Later, a situation arose when it was easier for foreigners to get citizenship of the country than for a citizen to get a membership of the CGC.

The value of CGC membership continued to appreciate with time. Eventually, it evolved into a kind of status symbol, like a privilege badge, a class in itself of the sort of peerage proportions, that was flaunted with a flair by its members in the higher rungs of social circles. Most men of consequence in the capital cherished this 'coat of arms' in undertones, not as such but in the name of legacy or rich tradition that the club membership supposedly signified. It served them as a tool to keep themselves distinct from those who have come closer to them using the device of democracy.

In the power corridors of the capital, whatever social station one might have reached if he is yet not issued a membership card of CGC, he still has a lot to achieve, without a mention. In the higher social circle of capital, many men of consequence felt inconsequential at the thought of not having a membership card of the CGC.

The newly born moneyed class which never missed a chance to flaunt its newly gained riches, often had their moment of epiphany when it was about gaining access into the gates of CGC. These plutomaniacs could have private pools, personal planes, and most expensive liquor flowing freely from the Magnum or Rehoboam at their mansions but not an entry into the club.

They certainly can pick up anything whatsoever is there in the market but at the doors of CGC, the realization that 'money cannot buy all things', often left them in lean humour. The further afterthought, that 'one thing out of all things' is membership of CGC, gave them heartburn. For an applicant seeking entry to the exclusive club, at one time the waiting period was more than two decades to graduate to the elite status of the CGC member. Anyway, unavailability adds to exclusivity and exclusivity to the social charm!

A few blocks away, the parliament is known to house a heterogeneous mixture of politicians who comes from far regions of the vast nation, naturally, they represent diversity but at CGC, like politicians, golfers too come in a classified assortment ranging from beginners to professionals; some are budding, others are blooming and few even bursting on the international circuits.

Members of CGC come from a cross-section of the population pool with diverse dispositions, and varied professional backgrounds, and carry large and lofty family legacies. They collectively contribute in the making of exclusive club culture that is unique to the club. They are of varying age groups from different walks of life; from dependent members who have just begun to walk to the super seniors who could barely walk. They also differ in their object of visit and motives for being a club member at all. Some come to play golf, some to soak in the fresh air, others for a tea tinged with club gossip, and some others drop in for they have nowhere else to go!

Some are morning visitors; others visit in the evenings. Some tramp in daily, others on weekends, and some others appear only once a year to vote and elect a committee. The golf course, however, is never devoid of action, it has its performers from the break of dawn till the balls begin to disappear in the darkness.

One can spot an assortment of golfing personalities performing at any given time in the course. It is easy to make out a band of 'exploders' who are easily identifiable with their explosive sound performances and shout effects. They often leave dug-up fairways behind, forgetting to fill the craters created by their clubs while they are on their onward journey in the game. 'Sulkers', swing from sullen looks to deadpan faces; a round gone bad for them means at least a day's sulking. Some of them may need an additional night's sleep after a tub of beer to get back into their routine life unless they play again and repeat the performance! If you find a man on a tee or a fairway simply waggling his club over the ball but unable to decide when to give it a shot, don't be surprised, he also is a golfer kind, often referred to as a 'waggler'. On golf greens if a man is twisting, turning, leaning, bending or crouching up for the fifth time, trying to line up his club in all possible postures but still missing the putt, he too is called a golfer, provided he paid his membership fee on time.

Still, regardless of all the chaotic characters that overrun its turf, CGC is a crucible for churning out golfing stars of national and international repute. It has opened its doors for the genuine seekers of the game. It has let the students of the game get to its ground and excel in the game irrespective of their background and social circumstances provided they proved to be the worthy claimant of golfing traditions. It has graciously opened its coffers to nurture young talent that exhibited the potential to reach the Claret Jug of Golf and raise it for the Club. Apart from club politics, golf is the other serious business that is undertaken seriously in its precincts.

Those for whom golf is still an alien sport may wonder, how could players of such varying proficiency in the game could coexist, play together and still enjoy the game, where some are professional practitioners of the skill while others could barely hit a ball straight. They need not to be surprised because the guild has devised a way of bringing all players on an equal playing parity while on the ground. The mechanism they employ to achieve this is called 'handicap' in golfing parlance. This saves the newbies from losing their spirits in the game, if not the balls, ensuring that they continue to cling to the fraternity.

The Capital Golf Club may be an overwhelming experience for someone alien to the club or the games played there but, in all earnestness, it is a true nursery for young golfers and also a shrine for a solemn seeker of the game.

No two golf courses in the world are alike! Each golf course is a unique layout as it is set in a unique environment which makes it distinct from others in its form, flow, and feel. However, it is not only layout and design that renders a distinction to a golf course, but also it has something to do with the golfers who golf there. In a club-course dwad, the two are bound to influence each other, and also determine each other's character. The local culture, customs, and people who dominate its turf also impart their imprint to a golf course.

Although a golf course is a prime asset for any golf club, golfers are the ones who form a club and play the course. Therefore, they influence the club culture significantly that evolve over a period of time. It is affected and accentuated by the cultural and social preferences of the members who join it.

Some golf clubs are known to be reserved and disciplined while others are open and inviting which evokes an immediate homely feel. Every club has its unique air and is known for its exclusive vibes, some are more engaging, while others are not. In some golf courses, the real fun begins only after the finish of the 18th green; starting from the 19th hole over drinks, settling wagers, exchanging arguments about the penalties, and musing about the odd pin position on a particular hole that had led to the bogey, and the loss of hole and consequently the wager! While some other clubs may have simple plain in and out vibes; you come, you play and you go.

The Club Culture

It was a cold and grey morning of a wintry Wednesday in December. The sky was smoky, blank, with no clouds and no Sun. In the hazy distance, the landscape, plants, buildings, and a group of golfers who were digging turf with their swinging clubs, all appeared as shades of grey, as if dusted with an ashen talc.

But, bit by bit the prospect brightened and the sunshine spread. Slowly as the visibility improved, the structures that were hidden in the haze began to develop in tones of vivid colours.

The Sun illuminated the turf and a treasure of pearls was revealed which had covered the entire course. Dewdrops glistened, balancing delicately on the tips of grass blades as if the goddess of riches had casually cast the gems from her purse. However, the attempt to gather them was in vain for they were gone at the slightest stir. Certain treasures are intended for everyone and are best beheld in eyes, verdant greens, and virgin nature at CGC are such treasures. To own such a treasure, one must walk to the riches every morning, golfers are however good walkers and so are blessed with them every morning.

The drops of dew that settled all over the turf during the night created a delicate watery canvas in the course. Even in the late morning, wet prints of golfer's walk and tire tracks of cruising golf carts were visible on the dewy turf of the fairways. Where all the early birds of golf ventured chasing their golf balls was obvious clearly from the art on the turf. It was easy to discern most marks, still, some eerie impressions were odd enough to pin them up to an acquainted inhabitant of the club with certainty. On the fairways, some strange prints of paws and wriggles of reptiles often left golfers guessing; before them, who could have had the guts to cross their turf in a cold windless night.

It was however dew, not rain, still wetness was all around. The pavements and the roads were wet. Under the trees, there was an occasional burst of shaken droplets which fell with a sudden perch of birds or a puff of wind. The canopy of the tea kiosks had gathered drops of dew, also tiny droplets that hung on the eaves of the club restaurant dripped drop by drop from the frills of awnings, with intermittent breaks as if of measured duration.

But irrespective of the weather, as always, the club was warm and inviting. The grey shade of the weather and its monotony were broken here and there with colourful blooms. A variety of winter annuals bloomed to their prime in December. Scrolls of Ice plants from the baskets swayed with the wind, which hung on the arm brackets and were fastened firmly to the lamp posts. The posts stood at equal distances, all along the driveway, entrance road, and paved path to the restaurant and clubhouse. Huge Dahlia bunches with wooden props were neatly showcased in painted pots. The winter blooms in perfect floral arrangements were placed at all major locations in the club, and as intended they enlivened the mood of all visitors in the dull December weather.

From the cafeteria of CGC, a savoury smell of hot servings floated freely in the vicinity. Strings of steam rose from the bowls of broth that were served on breakfast tables. Vapours escaping the breakfast lounge had a lingering peppery scent that enriched the surrounding air. The spicy savours of the soup seasonings and flavours from the hot pots of winter vegetables smelled blended and broke, all at once, as if competing to dominate one over the other. Coils of smoke from the clubhouse chimney rose above, as columns, and the steamy whiff from the exhaust vents of the cafeteria alluded to a horde of hale and hearty folks having a good time.

In those cosy shelters golfers and their families were enjoying the time of togetherness and vacations, it certainly was a time of merriment. The air was festive, Christmas was close and celebrations were on. The mood of the golfers was light and they lingered a little longer in the cafeteria.

However, a final call from the starter at the first tee made them move quickly, the moment they heard their names called they swung into action. Even if not done with their breakfast they grabbed a quick coffee from the shop and jumped onto their buggies zipping hurriedly towards the first tee with one hand on the steering wheel and the other in the pocket of their jacket, probing for warmth in the wet winter.

Manufacturers may prescribe the use of single foot while driving their golf carts but none encourage a one-hand drive. However, as they reached their destination with a one-hand and one-foot drive, their cart stopped with a jolt at a sudden press of the foot brakes. At this shaky stop, wavy-brown paper coffee cups that were held in holders of cart dash spilt their hot content through their lid spouts, staining the dash with a coffee splash.

It was an extra cleaning job for a caddy who clung and clambered over the strapped golf bags, steadying his feet on the fringe of the bag slot holder at the rear of the cart. Caddies know their golfers, the course, and their tasks very well. They are deft not only in their job of attending players' equipment but also in guiding them all through the course, right from the first tee to the finish of the round.

As cruising carts reached the starter's hut, caddies jumped off quickly. They pulled up a correct club from the golf bag with one hand, and a towel with the other, and as they walked a few steps after their masters to hand over a driver, the club face was already clean and shining. Caddies are agile beings, good at multitasking; by the time the golfers came back to their cart for their onward journey, the seat and its dash were spanking clean, again!

Not all golfers are fans of carts however, some preferred to walk too, they played the game the way it was invented and intended originally. Caddies shouldered their bags or pulled trollies with golf bags while golfers walked to the first tee, cradling a hot cup of steaming tea with both hands wrapped around it. Only the golfers knew better, whether they savoured the taste of the tea more or the warmth that the cup conveyed to them. In the cold, it is good to gather heat from wherever it comes because how a metal feels in winter mornings nobody knows better than a golfer who deals with their clubs each morning for several hours in the golf course.

At the scheduled time, the starter announced the names of the golfers and they ascended to the teeing ground turn by turn. The starter is there for every golfer at the first tee, he greets and makes everyone comfortable. He does his best to ease the nerves of each guest who is there to begin his game and the day, with a strike of a ball.

On the tee, a starter certainly sets the stage and mood for a golfer. He wishes every golfer to have a good start and a great round but not everyone hits the sweet spot of a golf ball to launch it high and lofty at his first strike of the day. Whether a player will have his drive nice and straight or the ball will shank into the forest depends purely on the player's performance and skills. Golf is not propelled purely by luck and wishes; it is about skills and hard work too.

The starter has to keep the show going for everyone in the course and so once a golfer and his ball leave the first tee he is on his own. Still, a player is never alone in his game. As a friend and guide his caddy is there with him throughout the four miles of forest and fairways in the game.

Golf course staff are often good multitaskers, if they are not initially, they become one over a period of time. It is necessary to keep up with the expectations of the golfers and the game. The starter is one such person in a golf course.

He is a kind of golf course concierge, who ensures that every golfer plays comfortably and has a memorable round on the course. He not only helps golfers start their game but also enlivens their spirit. At times he also turns out to be the only assistance to a golfer when his guest is in an odd situation and is not comfortable seeking assistance from any unacquainted staff of the club.

A golfer may overstretch his back muscles with the first swing of the morning, sometimes such severe stretching can lead to snapping of belt of his trousers, and even splitting of its seat is not an impossible scenario, if the wearing is too tight. It is the starter then who comes up as a first aid to a golfer in need with a quick massage on his back at a side bench or mending other serious breaches, thereby helping him stifle the moments of public embarrassment. A seasoned starter always keeps his supplies of lotions, painkillers and safety pins fulfilled.

He in essence is a multi-professionalist; for all sorts of situations happen when a golfer stretches left and right on the first tee to open up and begin his round for the day. Other than the role of therapist and tailor there are other varied skills that he often practices while sitting in his small shop. He has to make a match of golfers considering their common nature and preferences so that they can enjoy half of their day together on the course. However, his most important skill lies in maintaining pace of play in the course and ensuring everyone tees off on time.

The starter in a golf course is one of the closest acquaintances of every golfer. It is not only because every golf round starts on the clearance of Starter but there are several other reasons too. As golfers wait for their turn at the starter's hut, their casual conversations are often overheard by the starter who otherwise looks busy in his routine chores, these chunks of conversation may not make sense to the starter immediately but the bits of information when get collated in his head over a longer period of time makes an entire story. Thus, knowingly or otherwise golfers share a lot many secrets with the starter of the course they play often. Therefore in a club, a starter becomes one of the closest confidantes of golfers, and it is always safer to act friendly with someone who shares your secrets.

Amongst the golf course staff, the starter enjoys a privileged position in the eyes of the golfing patrons. Owing to the strategic station where he is placed and the unique job profile owing to which he is always in the vicinity of the golfers, the course starter is continuously enriched with the latest intelligence about everything that happens or is about to happen in the club, and therefore he serves as a repository of rich information.

Whenever golfers are in need of ammunition against their golfing rivals, they know where to look for and they try all tricks to woo the starter. However, being in the golf course for long, the starter knows exactly how to trade the stories without getting into the personal strife of golfers, and also who is a worthy seeker of such secrets.

The Club Keepers

Club members expect their club to be an ideal one. They want their golf course unblemished all through the year, in all seasons and at all times. At first thought, these expectations seem to be a basic bare minimum, the least one could ask for. However, keeping everything spot on in acres of limitless land spread all over, that too where nature keeps its clout, is not an easy task to accomplish. It further became a far-fetched dream in CGC, where each member expected his expectations to be met on an individual basis.

Further, the matrix of members at CGC consisted of golfers ranging from those in their teens to those who were in their nineties, some beginners and others professionals. Everybody had their own unique idea of an ideal club and wanted the course to suit their individual playing abilities. Therefore, even amongst the members, a consensus never existed on any matter of the club, some wanted the sand in bunkers to be soft and fluffy while others detested 'fried egg lies', for some the roughs were too long to get out while few others believed rough should be rough and challenging. Some were fans of the firm and hard fairways while others believed they didn't hold the ball properly due to which it rolls into the roughs. Striking a balance between the range of expectations was an unending pursuit for the superintendent and the secretary of the club.

Nevertheless, Olie and Stuart, the superintendent and the secretary respectively had put all their wits to work and earnestly aspired to meet everybody's expectations being the keepers of the club, but like a mirage, it was an ongoing chase, always. Irrespective of all the efforts of Olie and Stuart, members' cribbing never ceased. Though they dedicated their entire career in keeping the club to the best possible standards with available resources and existing constraints, how far they succeeded in keeping up the expectations of the members was hard to decide.

The challenge was not only about keeping the course as per members' expectations but doing so within the frame of the club's constitution. Following the book would have made their lives easy but if the duo tried to follow the club's constitution word-perfect, it inflamed several of the members whose convenience got in jeopardy. So the same members who sat in the committee formulating policies of the club to be executed by the office of the superintendent and secretariat, subtly issued vibes to go slow so as to suit the convenience of some of the privileged and powerful of the club. In the vicious circle of ethics and practicality, most often practically took precedence over pages of the club's constitution to ensure a normal pace of play in the club, and the game went on.

The very structure of the club was such that if word to word from the book were followed, its very existence might have landed in uncertainty. Some operational flexibility was necessary for the smooth functioning of the club and its employees. Going out of the way and serving the members of the club may not be prescribed in the club's constitution but most employees appeared inclined to appease their masters even if it was against the document. If Ms Parker wanted a little tending of her private lawns by the club's gardeners, Olie was obliged to send his boys to attend it without noise. If Ms Flores got a fancy for the new blooms in the club's nursery, how could the superintendent deny her such a trivial pleasure. If Mr Gardner has his guests visiting from abroad, and if he expected the secretariat to manage the tee time of his liking he was not asking for the world!

However, on all matters of the club, the final call was always of the secretary. He was empowered by the committee to decide in the larger interest of the club and was the authorized representative of the club management. However, authority is one thing and liking is another. In CGC, no member likes to listen to 'no' from the greenkeeper and the secretary, and if one is in power, in the committee, the club keepers are expected to come up with solutions to get things done, not excuses to say 'no' to members.

Olie and Stuart, therefore always attempted to keep members happy unless their demands fell completely off the frame of the club's constitution. In a democratic setup like CGC, there was no explicit 'Yes or No', but only exchange of favours. Wading through the political waters of the club was a tough task for Olie and Stuart as their responses never went without professional consequences.

In a club, where every member assumed the air of ownership of the club, respecting their demands on an individual basis demanded not only wits but also humility on the part of club keepers. Even on rare occasions when they were compelled to turn down the requests of club members the tone and tenor of expressing their regret mattered a lot. Individual survival was tough in the setup and so both of them knew that they had to be in it together.

The togetherness, however, was not there from the very beginning, it evolved over the years. In fact, about a decade ago when Stuart joined the club, the relations between Olie and Stuart began on odd terms. Stuart was strangely welcomed in his office on the very first day of his joining. He found an open book on his table, titled *'Letters to the Secretary'*, with a bookmark on a page that highlighted a text para reading, 'I got to know you are appointed the secretary, may heaven help you.' The message was clear enough, and Stuart quickly got a hang of what to expect in the club.

Stuart had a feeling that it was a mischievous attempt to scare him by Olie and his team. Initially, Olie might have tried to test the waters of the new secretary but as time went by he always was trumped by the skillfulness of Stuart. Olie eventually realized that the secretary was there to stay not only because he comes from the members' bloodline, but because he was educated and smart.

Stuart too realized that Olie was there for the last three decades and was going nowhere till he retires, he was like a permanent fixture in the psyche of the members whom he greeted every morning in the course, so an unspoken policy of parley struck between the two, which steadily evolved into a relationship of mutual coexistence with time. For them, it was not only important to scratch each other's back but also shield it from the members who always had something to complain about in the club. Also, over the years, they shared each other's secrets and got into an inevitable partnership to steer through the club politics in which a lone survival was not a practical proposition, and working against each other was absolutely out of the question.

Further, with the introduction of new technology and innovations in the green keeping trade and club management the old paradigms of club management were quickly transforming. Gone were the days, when Olie worked as an assistant to Simon who had wealth of experience and only experience was required to keep the turf green and members happy. Life was easier in those days, managing golf greens and the club was easier then, and most of the work was manual. In those days matters were not many, expectations were minimum, golf was a mere sport, there was no competition around no set standards, no benchmarks, and it was more about the experience than education.

But, by the time Olie had the reins of greenkeeping in his hands after Simon's retirement, his three decades of experience in growing grass began to fall short. Technology has disrupted the old norms and Olie began to lag behind the expectations of the members. The era of experience that worked fine for Simon had passed, now the world was already ushered in the era of the internet.

With the advent of technology, course management and the game of golf transformed quickly. From a mere sport, it grew into a sophisticated show. Olie and Stuart tried their best to catch up with the changes but in a committee club that is often high on expectations but slow on executions, members' expectations always exceeded the deliveries from the club keepers.

The committee however was aware that at CGC it was not only about keeping the greens but it was about keeping the club. The club was primarily striving to keep its members appeased, and with years of experience in the club set-up, Olie and Stuart were the real resources for such tasks. Therefore, in spite of all the routine verbal scuffles with the two, the committee always trusted the duo and valued them for their service to the club, though from the committee they seldom had their share of public appreciation and recognition.

In the club, there was nothing straightforward, all the matters were interwoven, which strand connects where in the club fabric was not obvious to every ordinary eye. Though, it was common knowledge that most members in the club were connected closely being kith and kin to each other, but at a particular time how distant they were in terms of their relations was not obvious to everyone.

For this fear, the staff mostly conversed cautiously about a member to the other in spite of all the coaxing that a member may employ to dig information about their distant relative and political rival in the club. The club was a conglomerate of lobbies, not one but sometimes multiple which were never in consensus about any matter of the club, their opinions always differed and attempts of making one lot of members happy often led to infuriating the other lot. Over the years, although Stuart had developed a discerning eye to see through the moods of the members, Olie in particular knew well when to talk and when to keep silent while engaging with members when they come up with their usual cribs and complains.

Olie's experience of dealing with members came in handy to Stuart in his initial days of joining the club, without his support he might have had struck a wrong nerve, landing himself in a deep rough of the club that had an overwhelming clan culture. Though Stuart commanded authority, he was unaware of the subterranean mines that existed everywhere in the club, an inadvertent stepping of which might have had blown him off from his seat of secretary had Olie not been there to supply him with the latest intel, and thereby enabling him nip the problems in the bud.

Olie was a great resource for the club and to Stuart too, for he had been there on the turf for more than three decades and knew exactly what is what and who is who; he knew at what address to send the boys for little tending of the lawns and where to send excuses. He knew where a few flower pots needed to be silently dropped and where to show the policy that states no outside sale of the club's plants.

Not only this, Olie always had an exact intelligence of what new alliances are in making in the club, which member is seeking the hand of whose son for his daughter and who is filing a divorce. He had the latest on how wide the rift between Fins and Finches has gone, and what Reeds and Ramos are up to with regard to their claim on alimony settlement. He could also relate if required about the issue of property division between Woods and Brooks. Or even what is going on in the circles of Parkers, Greens, Flores, or others with regard to the strategy of upcoming elections.

Nothing was secret for long in CGC, none knew who was being eavesdropped by whom; the waiter in the dining room, the starters on the first tee, the attendant in the lockers, or even the housekeeping staff cleaning the wash areas and pools. Who knows who is tipped by whom, and whose tips get higher to swing the loyalties of these discrete but free agents. Each staff shared an exclusive relationship with members, some were like masters to them while some others were just members of the club to a staff.

However, in committee clubs, as the committee and captain draw power from the membership, so do the employees. The larger the network base of members supporting a particular employee, the more the stability of the employee in the club, and the more the probability of his job security. Olie certainly had served his masters more closely and keenly for the longest durations, and so was well placed in the club. Therefore, in times of professional crisis, he had several levers to pull and multiple buttons to press.

However, the special agent services of the club staff were only to their specific masters, not for all. The news and rumours in the club had value to the club members and so the staff often felt compelled to quickly dispose it to their favourite members who might gain something out of it. In lieu of these errands they never expected much, the tips and Christmas gifts which they received as per the occasion, however, were a mere token of appreciations from the members for their routine services which they couldn't refuse out of courtesy.

An obligation is a by-product of getting a service out of order. Though such obligations are not obvious to the people around, the obliged and the obligated however remember the favours. Olie as an old greenkeeper was a known face to every member of the club and also, he had been quick in attending to the needs of all influential members, sometimes even going out of the way to please his masters, consequently he thrived on a strong support base of the members. Although, professional hazards exist everywhere, and CGC was no exception but still Olie was gifted in keeping multiple members to his side. It was a talent necessary to survive in a members' club and Olie was amply endowed with the skills.

The Committee

Golf Clubs in general are either private properties where a buck stops at the owner or committee clubs where the buck never stops. The most interesting aspect of committee clubs is their committees. A club committee in simplest terms is a group of members who have enough time, energy, and heart to volunteer themselves for furthering the cause of the golf club, pro bono.

Mostly they are the members from the golfing pool itself who have got everything and now expect no more from the world outside. They seem to be indifferent to the happenings outside the club's boundary, spending most of their time in the club as if trying to serve the god through his game.

However, in a club, everybody has their opinion about everybody else in the club. The restaurant staff of CGC, therefore, kept an altogether different opinion on this matter too, they said member contests for the committees when their wives cease to pick up their phones and children start issuing excuses to evade their petty pestering at home.

They argued that pursuing the same track that too with the same fourball every day is not life, for everybody! After all their families too have their lives to live. When the families of these whiners are fed up and they begin to experience the daily disparage at their homes, they get into the club committees to find a bunch of other people called club staff, to vent out their exasperation.

CGC was a committee golf club; a public club predicated on public land and politics. But politics in the club was not like the one in the parliament, a couple of blocks away, here it was practised with grace and eloquence.

The politics here was cultured and cultivated in its finest form; here it was not only kept alive but healthy too. Nobody in the club escaped its effect as it was nurtured in every nook and cranny of the club premises. If someday politics dries out in the national parliament, CGC could easily serve as a national reserve for politics.

Politics is the only tool in a democracy to retain power and so every man of means in CGC aspired to excel in the art. It was late afternoon, and the fourball of Mr Green was heading towards the tee. The Starter came out from his hut promptly, a gesture of paying special regard to an important member of the club.

He greeted the group with a smile and elicited a conversation. Further, on a subtle prompting from the fourball, he recounted the discussions of morning golfers, elaborating in detail about their opinions on the club and its functioning. He also related the opinions of some evening golfers as per whom Mr Mark was a preferred choice of most members for the upcoming election for club captaincy. In the end, he summed it all up with his own personal opinion subtly suggesting that Mr Mark should certainly contest for the club captain in the upcoming elections, pleasing Mr Mark and his fellow golfers.

Mr Mark Green was one of the most active and energetic members of the club's Green Committee. He was young and had an exceptional eye for detail, and a flair for learning everything. But at present he was on his pursuit of mastering the skills of greenkeeping. To his fellow players, he pointed out a patch of discoloured grass at the corner of the tee suggesting that it was a fungal infection that if not checked quickly would spread in the entire course. He then pulled his cell phone out and called the course superintendent, Mr Olie, instructing him to treat the patch on priority and also drawing his attention to a few weed sprouts at the margin of the first tee.

The message was delivered to not only Olie but also to a few other members who were there around the tee and the nearby putting green, people noted the concern of Mr Mark for the course and his dedication to the club, precisely as intended. After all, he is an aspiring captain of the club, and he is serious about the course upkeep.

At one time, Mr Mark was one of the promising golfers of CGC, a spirited one. He was sure to shine as a pro golfer on the tour until the fateful summer afternoon when he drove himself into a culvert at the 13th hole while having a spirited round after having a few beers on the go. When he recovered from the fractures and the shock, he realized that he had lost his swing. He however claimed that on that fateful day, he got distracted by a sight of a screeching green mower machine on the adjacent fairway which led him to lose track, and ever since has been blaming unprofessional green keeping practices practised in the club for killing away a future golfing star.

Mr Mark was a man of motivation, when his dream of making a mark as a golfer on the pro circuit was dashed by the high decibels of the green mower, he vowed for a change. He resolved to change the manner in which his club functions and more so to professionalise the greenkeeping department of his club.

Along with motivation, he was also a man of means, for he was the grandson of one of the wealthiest founding members of the club. His father, uncles, and brothers all have already served as Captain or President of the Club in the past. Naturally, the common cogs and wheels of the club were at his disposal and he could have wrenched up some of the screws of the greenkeeping department with a little fiddling from behind the veil.

However, in spite of his family stronghold in CGC, he knew that the club is public and in a democratic dispensation no act should appear personally motivated, particularly if one has ambitions of being at the helm of the organization. So he decided to take the task head-on and follow the traditional track of service, the safest and surest route to reach the top in democracy.

He further felt strongly for club service when he realized that with the surgery of his arm following the recent mishap, outshining his fellow friends in professional golf would be an impractical proposition, instead, he could reach the Club Honour Roll easily with a routine round of golf at his home club. So he began to work for the good of the game and the club, emulating his father and the family.

Furthermore, greenkeeping is perceived to be a technical trade with a supposedly scientific basis, so to be sure and safe he decided to have a backing of some qualification before tinkering with the greenkeeping department or at least be there in the Green Committee to have an authority of command. Driven with a desire to leave a mark in the club's chronicle, he soon acquired both, a garb of greenkeeping qualification and a seat in the boardroom.

He had a crash course in greenkeeping from the USA that made him comfortable in pronouncing scientific names of a few fungicides and a hang of some turf tending techniques like topdressing, aerification, and verticutting. For him, this much in conjunction with a tag of a committee member was enough to crush even the famed agronomists of the turf industry. In any case, he got an edge over other committee colleagues, and so he was always listened to with heightened curiosity and regard.

Mark and his fourball finished their game and were just settling at the clubhouse when a member came cribbing. He was arguing about the status of newly dug flower beds along the fairways which were left unmarked, whether it was GUR and so a free relief or an integral part of the course where the ball was to be played as it lies. Seeing Mark, a committee member, they came straight to him asking for clarification. He pulled his phone and called the concerned people to have an immediate clarification as the matter could have escalated, the group involved was always on bets and such errors in course setup led to heated arguments sometimes escalating to ugly fights amongst such fourballs in the golf course. Though, most often the group involved was known to have its common bill of breakfast for the day at stake!

Golf courses may differ but people say, the world over the committee golf club members are alike. If you ask who these people are, then the secretary and the superintendent are the people who seem to be largely unified in this kind of opinion. When asked in private, they say that committee members are super fault finders. They always have something to tell, especially about what is wrong with the course they just walked in. They walk out the eighteenth green grumbling, finding faults with greens, their partners, caddies and sometimes even with the game of golf itself!

They always find the grass greener on the other course across the street and have handy tips for their own greenkeeper. They fancy themselves to be an accomplished golfer by the very virtue of being a member of the golf club. They believe firmly that the ball that did not drain into the hole, in the first putt, has something to do with the firmness of the putting green and the skills of the greenkeeper maintaining it! To a passing greenkeeper, they sometimes pitch out their greenkeeping insight as banter but many a time the tone is direct and dictating.

A committee club golfer cannot imagine a day in his life where he does not have his fourball or has no golf or its talk at the least. He finds his daily solace only at the course or at the club's bar. Members who have had their hair grow grey, walking the same track every day since the time they were kids, cannot be separated from their home club for more than a few days without withdrawal symptoms. It may be difficult to explain, but topophilia is a sure thing! People and places do bond, and the repetition in the case of golfers must be more aggravating.

The members of the CGC club claim that the golf club is their second home but if need be, they can forsake their first home for the second, for it is the golf course where they spend all of their wakeful hours. Late at night when they step out of the pub they are numb and when they wake up to their senses in the morning, their drivers deposit them back onto the club's turf. In fact, some members are so lost in the ambience of the club and its bar that it is only at late night when they see an incoming phone call from their wives, that they realize they have another home too.

A golfer, or for that matter a golf club member breaks into the starters area, even before a break of dawn; tees off, talks, walks, and breakfasts somewhere in the midway and after about a half a day of defeats and conquests, flags-in at the 18th green. In the other half, they crib and complain over the first half.

To have some discrete means to blame for all their first-half miseries, and ensure the continuity of this two-half order of daily life unabated, each year they religiously appoint a committee in charge of the greens. The Green Committee once constituted, meets; and meets frequently. The meetings are elaborate, grand; and sometimes epic for they are expected to plan, master plan; and decide the present and future course for their club.

However, ironically enough, even after rounds after rounds of meetings, decisions are not made. There is a common joke that does the rounds in CGC, that in the boardroom discussions keep going in circles because for meetings the committee sits at the round table, and for this, it is not the committee who is to be blamed but the club's interior designer!

People wonder why decisions are made seldom when meetings are held so often in the boardroom of CGC. Interestingly, some very successful people with high business acumen are the ones who constitute committees in these golf clubs. But surprisingly when they sit together in a golf clubs' boardroom they often fall short of adding up to the sum of apparent parts. They individually head big multinational ventures, steering groups of some of the brightest minds of the country in their own private companies. But, when it is about making a collective decision in a golf club boardroom, the agenda is mostly carried forward meeting after meetings; sometimes several years down the line, the succeeding committees discuss the same points as were deliberated upon by their predecessors.

Irrespective of everything else, members of the club gather annually for the electoral celebrations to eat, play and vote. The newly elected members constitute the General Committee of the club, which gives rise to several sub-committees, including the Green Committee. A new committee in a golf club is like a new hope, a hope of change, it comes with a resolve to reform.

But who wants reforms in a democratic setup? Certainly, the majority, those who don't appreciate the existing setup. And who is authorized in a democracy to reform the existing setup? The existing setup! A vicious circle of hope and hurdles, therefore, continues year after year.

A Green Committee has a typical three stages in its one-year life cycle. Let's change, let's try to change, and we should change. Eventually, a year passes, the committee changes and two-half order of committee club members' life remain unchanged. Committees come and committees go, but golfers and the game remains, and so does its glory!

Like most committee golf clubs, the Green Committee of the Capital Golf Club has about a dozen representatives. The membership elects a new set every year by exercising their suffrage. The elected committee members are then allotted a mailbox, a reserved parking space and a right to attend meetings, formally. In a speakeasy air, they could also now freely boast themselves as the club's custodian at the bar.

Within the first few days of its own birth, the General Committee, with its dozen members, interestingly hatch into a batch of two dozen subcommittees. A chairman in one committee may act as a co-chairman in the other or can chair multiple committees, or exist just as a member in a subcommittee. The GC is not only divided into the apparent subcommittees, but also into subgroups that are visible only to the ones who watch the entire election in entirety, and later the action of the boardroom closely and in detail.

Elections are seldom between individuals but are between ideologies or groups, the individuals may appear united in structure but the rift of ideologies remains. It's human to develop a preference for one over the other, especially when one has a choice to choose. All may not participate in the electoral process per se, but almost everybody lobbies for one or the other group. This group identity creeps into the boardroom too, and the GC has members not only from the captain's lobby but also from the opposition. The captain exercises his creativity in creating sub-committees and the portfolios of preference generally go to the members of his own group; nothing in the constitution of the club holds him from exercising his free will while deciding its constituents.

Anyway, the multiple sects created in the name of subcommittees give enough opportunities to the committee members to keep meeting at the pretext of one or another club matter. Also, in case they decide anything in a subcommittee, they have all the chance to undecide it in the General Committee when they all sit together every month, and interestingly they hardly miss that opportunity.

However, in a golf club, golf is the primary pursuit and the golf course is the key object of discussion. The captain of the club chairs the Green Committee and so he is accountable to the members and the committee. But unlike other committee members, the secretary and the superintendent are the only two paid and permanent members of the committee who generally last for more than a year and so they are held accountable for everything that happens and even for that which doesn't happen in the club; by the members, the committee, and the captain.

The Boardroom

Mr Stuart, the secretary, was there in his office a little early on the day. Setting up of the boardroom was almost over; against each seat, bottles of water and tissue trays were laid neatly on the large oval table, lights were switched on, the computer projector setup was ready, and the office attendants were in a hurry to clear the room before the arrival of green committee members.

As the needles of the post-clock mounted at the entrance circle began to race for their eleventh lap tracing its golden dial, activity in the car parking lot picked up. One after the other, cars of all colours began to pile up at the reserved bays of committee parking. Fog lights of the cars gleamed in all directions at the spot during the momentary rush as drivers manoeuvred their vehicles. The engines and the lights turned off, following which fine gentlemen in their formal winter attire were seen alighting and proceeding towards the administrative block with quick steps.

The corridors of the boardroom which were cold and desolate a few minutes ago began to warm up with the arrival of committee members. All the gentlemen were admitted in, and the doors of the boardroom clicked shut for a scheduled Green Committee meeting. The attendance was in full. Obviously, some urgent matter was on the agenda as most members arrived a few minutes earlier than they were normally used to.

The boardroom is considered closed when the doors are shut. All committee members are privy to the matters discussed in the boardroom but the discussions are deemed confidential until the minutes of the meetings are signed, circulated, and published. Each year as soon as the election results are out, the secretariat dispatches invitation and induction kits to every elected member that includes policy papers enunciating such expectations, though not explicitly. Therefore, nobody doubts the honourable members of the committee but the walls had never been reliable keepers of secrets, they have a history of breaches. Also, who doesn't know that walls too have ears, don't they?

To keep things less complicated, the boardroom of CGC has the simplest clutter-free interiors. It has a round table with a set of 12 chairs, a large-sized TV screen, and a gold-green rimmed Rolex timepiece mounted on the wall adjoining the common corridor. Time has a special place in the game of golf, one can find all kinds of golfers on the course, even the late finishers but rarely one who fails to start on time. To ensure golfers keep up with time, the Swiss timekeeper itself has taken the responsibility of keeping time for golfers.

Rolex got into a relationship with golf about half a century ago, and since then it has been installing its signature golden-green clocks at all strategic locations in the club including the starting tee, or next to the starter's hut. Now the tee-off time is decided by the clock at the tee and not by the watch on the player's wrist; and at the tee, time means on the dot! This saves penalties for players and time for the starter, which otherwise would have been lost in arguments over time.

The Swiss clockmakers claim that it's the timeless tradition and values of the game, for which they care, and so continue to serve golfers. However, their actual service is to the non-golfers, the first-time visitors to a golf course, who know nothing about golf and its weird landmarks; the 7th hole, at the midway hut, next to the starter hut, in the back nine, under a tree on the 8th, and so on. These unique Post Clocks serve as a solid landmarks for worldly beings. Over the years these clocks have become a kind of time emblem, owing to which a golf event gets etched in time, in the memory of visitors, perhaps serving the actual purpose for which the relationship exists!

In CGC, a two-dial Rolex Post Clock stands on the first tee, a four-dial at the main entrance near a roundabout, and its single-faced sibling keeps ticking for the committee in the boardroom. The green Rolex clock mounted on a wall just above a large TV screen in the boardroom announced eleven, and as the casual stir across the large round table settled, the Captain and Chair began formally.

'Gentlemen, Welcome! Before Secretary begins business for the day, I wish to brief the committee on the latest proceedings about the crucial court case that has been going on for more than a decade now, regarding the 18th green land dispute. As it's nearing its final hearing, I and the Secretary have been busy in it all this while.'

The captain continued, 'I am told that during the last hearing, our claim for the 18th green land parcel didn't fare well in the court. Unfortunately, the Club is not in very good standing on this, the documentary evidence is in Bob's favour. The final verdict may come anytime and the only option to solve it appears to be out of court for which Mr Bobby doesn't seem to agree. Bob appears to have taken it as a matter of personal ego as all our previous attempts of negotiating with him have been without any luck! However, as per the decision in the last Open House meeting, a core group of a few senior and influential members of the club is constituted. The group is scheduled to meet Bobby this Saturday to convince him and negotiate formally. We are trying our best to save the 18th green, but we have our fingers crossed until some real breakthrough is made. We hope the core group succeeds in its attempt to settle the matter out of court as the time is running out.'

After listening to the captain's commentary in silence, the discussion in the boardroom got split into subgroups, and a general murmur pervaded. Those who were new to the committee tried digging details of the issue from others who were more informed about the matter. Since the time the matter was disputed in the court of law, the minutes of the meetings of the green committees had been having a continuous mention of the dispute along with the progress made in that regard year after year. However, most casual members care primarily about their tee times in the club unless they are on the committee. And so, most new members of the committee had lost track of the chronology of the long-drawn lawsuit, especially how and when it all began.

The story of the 18th green land dispute in short was about two close friends, Mr Bob and Mr Billy, and their fat egos. Though for almost a decade now, they had been holding rivalry against each other sumptuously, but prior to that, they shared a deep bond of friendship which was passed to them from a generation before them in legacy.

The fathers of Mr Billy and that of Mr Bobby were friends in the good old days, in the days when the new City Planning Act came up. Large-scale infrastructure development was due in the capital city. This was an era when their friendship further got fortified, for they had an opportunity to work together. Late Mr Archer, the father of Bobby was a businessman with great acumen and foresight, and sensing the opportunity he developed his interests in real estate too. Incidentally, Late Mr Green, Billy's father, was a key government bureaucrat involved in the project in those days. He was the chief person responsible for the execution of the new city development plan. All the major development that happened under the scheme was overseen by him; in that period of time, he was the main man behind the transformation of the capital.

Billy and Bobby's fathers were a fan of the game of golf too which was introduced to the elite circle of the society by the Scots. However, in those days they used to practice their newly gained golfing skills with some of their Scottish friends at an older turf track near a racecourse. Further, as per the new master plan of the capital, a central university was to come up where the old course existed. Billy's father, being at the helm of affairs in the government, got approval to shift the old course to a new location. Eventually, the blueprint of the new city also had a place for a new golf course, thus the Capital Golf Club came into existence at its new and present location.

However, to fit the course layout perfectly, a small pocket of adjoining land was required that fortunately was in the name of Late Mr Archer. This being not a big deal for the golfing friends, he immediately handed over the land parcel to the club for their mutual golfing interests. Thereafter, on this pocket of land, a sprawling 18th green and a classic clubhouse of CGC came up. Legally, however, it was never transferred to CGC on papers, there being no need in those times. Therefore, as per land records, it was still in the name of Bobby's family.

Unable to make much out of the murmur in the boardroom, Mr Richie Parker said, 'Can the Chairman, please brief about the background of this case in a little more detail for the benefit of members like me who are in the committee for the first time and are not very familiar with the background of the case, and it sounds to be a very crucial a matter for the club.

The captain said, 'Indeed it is a crucial matter, though I know a fair deal about it, however, it all began in the Secretary's office, and in front of Stuart, so I think he will be able to relate it better.'

Picking a gesture from the captain, Stuart began the story, 'We know that Mr Billy our present president and Mr Bob grew up playing this course together, however, it was a new year party eve, about a decade ago, in which a colleague of Mr Bobby came along with him as his guest. The party continued till late at night and his guest who was not a golfer got out of the party area to talk on his cell phone and sat on a golf cart parked in the proximity, and probably under the sway of the spirits drifted to a nearby open area next to the clubhouse. Absorbed in his conversation he kept on taking circles in the open, by the time a Security staff spotted the whirling cart in the dark on the green, it was too late!

'The next morning, there were only tyre marks and no putting green. A temporary green was immediately created so that the game could continue as the 18th green was then Ground Under Repair. The then Captain, Mr Billy took cognizance of the matter seriously and said, "those who do not care for the tradition of the golf club and cannot care for the course must be taught a lesson to teach them how to behave in a golf course". He suspended Bobby's membership for as long as the grass didn't grow back on the green, for bringing unruly guests to the golf course. Probably, the suspension was too much of an embarrassment for Bob, the grass on the green recovered in a few weeks but relations between Bob and Billy never did. Nobody knows the real reason for the rift but since then the two friends were never seen playing together. Bobby built a golf course for himself but also filed a case claiming 18th green as the land parcel was in his family's name.'

Stuart concluded and sucked a breath.

Mr Mark, however, seemed not satisfied with the version of the story that Stuart narrated.

He added, 'But to bring the story in perspective, the committee should also know that it was the casual approach of the Secretariat towards club affairs that led to the 18th green dispute. A decade ago, the invite that was sent to members from Stuart's office on the fateful New Year's Eve was not worded correctly which led to confusion, eventually. Had he pronounced the terms clearly in the card, Bobby would have not brought his guest to the club and no further complications would have occurred.'

Sir, the invite clearly said 'Member and a plus one'. Stuart argued that 'plus one' by default means wife or a date, not any random friend!

Mark, refuted quickly, 'But the secretary's job is to simplify things and communicate in Black and White English, without leaving any chance for a grey area, not everybody is a language buff to understand every English phrase and its subtle meanings.

'Also, you didn't mention that it was not only Bobby who didn't return to the club but also the Minutes Keeper. His key staff, who was in charge of the club's record-keeping and document archives also went missing, that too with an only ancient document that had a written mention of the land parcel gifted to CGC by Bobby's father. You failed not only to retain the old staff who was privy to all sensitive information but also to protect such a sensitive document which could have turned the case in our favour. It was surely a lackadaisical attitude of Sturt, an error of the Secretariat, which aggravated into larger complications jeopardizing the very interests of the Club. It could now cost the entire green 18th, and the esteem for the club.'

Sensing the escalation of arguments further between Mr Mark and Stuart, the Chairman quickly interjected to give a different turn to the discussion and said, 'Secretary, you may now please proceed with the agenda of today's meeting.'

The secretary was looking for such an escape, as he knew very well that there is no advantage in proving his point against a member of a committee, especially if the member is also a brother of Mr Billy, who is at the core of all the dispute and also a serving president of the club.

Stuart proceeded with the business of the meeting and said, 'Agenda Item No.1 is Review of Golf Course

Conditions. We received a consignment of "Revolution and Magic Drops" fertilizers that are imported from Hono Lulu, last week as per the recommendations of our Course Consultant Mr Hunt from Grow Green Consultant, and we shall be fertilizing our greens this week. We are hopeful that greens will improve within a fortnight and conditions.'

Mr Mark interrupted him again, 'We need a revolution in the methods we function in this club, so as to get things done quickly and improve our sinking golf course, rather than throwing our money on fancy foreign fertilizers from Hono Lulu.'

Mr Parker voiced a similar opinion and said, 'The Club is slowly slinking down, its reputation is sliding and nobody seems serious enough to keep up its reputation, which many generations have toiled for. In my forty years of playing golf, I had never seen such pathetic course conditions'. He concluded with a thump on a big oval table of the boardroom and a scornful look at Olie.

Mr Mark snapped in again, 'True, I absolutely agree with you Richie!'. He retained the focus of the committee and conversation to himself and kept the ridicule rolling across the table to the secretary and the superintendent.

Mr Parker, however, seemed not to give a lead to Mr Mark in steering the conversation. He said, 'Our course is no more a course; it is reduced to something like a municipality park. If one wants to understand the difference between a golf course and a park, one should walk across the street and see what golf courses are like. This weekend greens of Divine Luxury were stimping at 13 plus, how can they maintain such perfect conditions but not us.'

Out of the dozen members in the committee of CGC, only a few remain active participants in the routine committee meetings, most others occupy the chairs as silent spectators. It was obvious that those who raked the issues and criticized the current conditions of the course most are the ones who have something in their minds. They were the ones who in all probability were the future contestant for the club captaincy in the next year's elections. Criticising the present and projecting self as a solution is a time-tested approach followed by all who rose to power through elections in any democratic setup. Thus, Mr Mark and Mr Riche Parker's competing attempt to criticize the course was natural and obvious.

Mr Mark carried the argument of Mr Parker further, he said, 'I absolutely agree with Richie, our maintenance standards have sunk drastically. The entire club is in tatters and the secretary has so much to attend to if he cares for secretarial affairs rather than assuming Superintendent's role and suggesting what 'drops or magic drops' should be sprayed for growing grass, which certainly is Olie's job.'

Mark had a tinge of anger against the secretary, for he was the one who had mismanaged the entry of Bobby on the New Year's Eve that led to the consequent clash of Bobby and his brother, Bill. Eventually prompting Bobby to raise the claim for the 18th green.

In undertones, the membership blamed Billy for not dealing with the matter delicately and letting it escalate to such extremes. Since the time Bobby's threats about the 18th green got real, the membership's electoral favours shifted from Greens to Parkers, and since then the club has seen more captains from the lines of Parkers than Greens.

The boardroom of Capital Golf Club has been a witness to many generations of golfing members metamorphosing from committee members to chairman. Traversing slowly from the farthest corner of the round table, passing and progressing before being able to reach the central throne of Chairman's chair.

However, in spite of being on the committee for the first time, Mark, a young scion of the Greens lineage was aspiring to become the next captain. He was hardworking and dedicated to the cause of the club but he understood that the voting share could swing in his favour only if he or his family could succeed in resolving the matter of the 18th green.

In most committee meetings, especially the ones nearing the tail end of their tenures, hardly anybody listens to what others are saying, other than the minute-takers and voice-recorders. However, this committee was new and was in its first stage of 'let's change', therefore discussions continued and most members were attentive throughout the meeting. A light lunch was ordered in the late noon, and post-lunch the meeting resumed again.

The meeting turned out to be a marathon, epic one, and when all agenda points were exhausted with no other point for discussion, the meeting concluded with a vote of thanks dispersing in the late afternoon.

The Secretariat

At the second story of the administrative block, the Boardroom and the Secretary's office were hardly a few steps apart. A narrow common corridor connected the two, and in between existed a few cubicles of clerks that flanked the Financial Comptroller's chamber. In the corridor, several golf-landscape arts in neatly bevelled matted frames were hung. Some of the signature holes and picturesque locations of the golf course were showcased vividly in oil and paint.

On the white walls of the narrow gallery, the pictures were unmissable by the first-time passers-by and so was the artist's signature on them, an etch of heavy strokes. The art pieces bore not only the initials of the artist but his club's membership number too, an indication of an in-house attempt.

The gallery also had sections of glass shelves showcasing its cherished possessions; an old featherie, along with some ancient guttys, and antique woods and metals. The playing tools of the past generation were donated by the present golfing lot of the club and preserved for everyone as a collective treasure of golfing history on display. Further, in a small recess of the wall stood a full-length locker mailbox, each box of which was captioned with the name of the GC member, to whom it was allotted.

From the ground floor, rose a case of winding stairs that culminated at the doorway at the 2nd storey; right at the face of Miss Tia. The reception was well lit with an inbuilt desk lighting which was further complemented by an illuminating smile of Miss Tia, who sat there and greeted cheerfully every incoming visitor. Adjoining the reception was the office of the secretary, the first room on the right of the corridor and on the left was the captain's chamber.

However, the office chamber of the secretary was a spacious, comfortable medium-sized room. The other side of the room was a half-wall and half-window. The window panes running from the boardroom to the secretary's office all in a continuum formed the outer facade of the administrative block. The glass panes of the secretary's office window spanned from the floor to the ceiling, cased in a hinged frame that tilted to let the fresh air in, or when the Secretary sought to pick the conversations of the golfing groups at the close by first tee or practice putting green.

Though, sometimes deciphering low decibels of silent whispers in entirety might have been difficult, yet, he always succeeded in gathering the gist of it. Howsoever feeble the feel of floating gossip may be, he often was able to guess exactly what all was being cooked in the minds of the members at the first tee of the club. Because being the secretary of the club, he had all the details of the golfers at his disposal, to collate with what he witnessed from his office window in real time.

The incoming sunlight that entered the room was not only modulated by the tinted glass panes of the window but also filtered first by a thick crown of an evergreen tree that stood just a few feet from the building.

The tree thrived profusely and the natural spread served as a camouflage for the secretary's secret window, keeping it off from the eyes of the passing golfers. The branches not only served the purpose for the secretary but also gave shade to the passers-by therefore they were let to have a luxuriant growth, but sometimes when the offshoots tried to intrude in his office through the window, a pruning was inevitable.

The natural light entering through the window was further softened by a beige blind which blended beautifully with cream colour of the interior of the walls. Along the length of the window wall lay a downy sofa that was a favourite seating spot for visitors not only because of the comfort but for the view it offered.

The interiors of the secretary's office were designed in a chic style with an urban modern theme with all the ergonomics considered and thought out. The elements in the room were all smooth and soothing so as to keep the Secretary at ease, leaving little room for complaints from his side. After all, he was the one entrusted with the job of resolving complaints of the club, and how he could have a reason to complain! The secretary was the main representative of the club to the inner and outer world. The office of the secretary of such a club is expected to reflect the grandeur of the club, and Stuart's office with all the modern means and materials with which it was furnished, did so appropriately.

The AC was centralized, a radiator stood in alignment with a sidewall, and a decent-sized walnut desk with a glass tabletop lay in the centre. On top of the table at the left corner were placed a to-do-slip pad, a leather cover planner, and a cup of pens with a stapler hung on its lip at its hinge. On the other corner rested a miniature laughing Buddha with a Lucky Bamboo bonsai.

On the back wall was a velour pinboard, with a coloured course map having its ornate compass rose in the top right corner. At one side of the board was tucked a neatly printed Excel Sheet of the tournament calendar for the next few months. The foot of the back wall had a low-rise cabinet counter that had a Printer and a few Club's Yearbooks stacked on it. On his left return sat a sleek laptop computer with a couple of books and booklets. At the foot of the return was an electric paper shredder, and a neat paper dustbin under the desk on his side. The desk also had a button for an electric call bell.

At an angle stood a stout mahogany gilt-brass mounted gueridon on which lay a sleek ceramic camphor burner. It burnt in a soft glow, illuminating the stack of books by its side; Club's Constitution and Bye-Laws, and a pair of R&A-USGA Official Guide to the Rules of Golf along with its Player's Edition booklet. Next to the books, a framed certificate of the Club's USGA membership was displayed, inclined on a cardboard easel back.

The desk was complemented with an ergonomic emerald leatherette chair for the secretary and a pair of matching visitor chairs on the other side of the desk. On the front wall a large TV screen was mounted, that either played Golf TV or displayed the feed of multiple CCTVS installed in the club. The grid view covered live footage right from the Kitchen of the Dining Room to the First Tee of the Club. So, the secretary sitting in his office knew exactly what had been served to a particular member, what he munched and what he left. If he was not too busy, he could even tell you what effect it had on that day on his drive at the first tee. For he not only has the feed of cameras at his disposal but also the strategically located window that gives a live view of the first tee and the performances made there.

When the window blind was gathered aside, one can have a clear view of the outer panorama from the height. The main Club entrance, the first tee with Starter's hut and a large practice putting green left to the tee, all in a single span of sight. The committee members' parking was also in clear view, so the secretary knew exactly who was out there in the course and what kind of a complaint to expect that day.

At CGC, each golfer has his unique set of perennial complaints with regard to the golf course, and the same was true for committee members too, irrespective of their graduation to the board. One committee member always found faults with the bunkers, and so consequently the greenkeeping crew nicknamed him Mr Sandy. For him, someday the bunker sand was wet, the other days it was too dry, some other days it was too shallow or too deep. Some others had their expert views on forest management while few others were born landscapers. There were also members who always cribbed about the speed of the greens. With a long experience with the golf club, golfers and its committees, Stuart always kept his specific team ready on all days to attend to the expected complaint based on the car parked in the reserved lot.

However, about a decade ago the office of the secretary was not the same when Stuart joined the Club. It used to be a small obscure chamber in a section of the maintenance complex, a few yards from the Superintendent's office where most action happened. The old secretariat which essentially was a part of the superintendent's office, adjoining the chamber of the secretary were few cabins of the clerks who existed there to assist the secretary in his routine works which were minimal. In those days the secretary's role usually included relationship management with the members, playing a round of golf and attending queries which were few, and meetings which were fewer.

The clerks were there to help the secretary with keeping records of the accounts and membership, however, most secretarial jobs were often looked after by the superintendent, who was there on the course most of the time while the secretary seldom visited his office chamber for whenever he visited the club he was mostly found playing in the course, he being a member himself.

In those days, there was a tradition of honorary secretaries, so they changed every year with the Captain, President, Treasurer and the committee. The title of honorary secretary probably served them primarily one purpose; to get the tee-off time of their choice.

When golf began in the capital, and began the tradition of honorary secretaries, it must have begun in earnest. So in those days, the incentive for honorary secretaries might not be the preferential tee-off time but their genuine interest in the game and the pride they must have taken in promoting the larger cause of popularizing golf in the Capital.

Because in its formative days, not many people visited the golf course and getting a tee time was not a task, but getting a full fourball certainly was. Even in the capital, very few had the money and time to play golf. As time went by, residents of the capital grew wealthy and golf came within the reach of middle class. Membership of CGC swelled steadily and then getting a tee-off time of choice became a privilege amongst the privileged. Therefore, this might have been one of the motivations for being the secretary of the club in the early days.

However, the need for a permanent secretary was felt as the membership grew, it was obvious from the committee minutes of that era that had a repeated mention of having a full-time secretary in several of its meetings. Particularly the voice to hire a new full-time secretary appears emphatic in the recorded minutes of the meetings after the movement of the old superintendent. Mr Simon, the then superintendent had retired owing to his old age passing his office to Olie, who starting as his steno had helped him some 30 years in various roles.

A requirement for a full-time paid secretary and Simon's replacement became imminent within a year or so of his retirement. The void created by the absence of an experienced Superintendent, and an open-door secretariat was reflected in the overall dismal standard of the golf course conditions and its functioning during that period, and after long stretched deliberations spanning several committees, finally, a committee with a captain came who eventually got an ad published for the position of secretary.

Several applications were reviewed but the most relevant appeared to be that of the then captain's own nephew, Mr Stuart. He not only had a newly popular MBA degree in his hands from a foreign university but also had played golf being from a golfing family. Who else could have been a better fit, if not him?

As a young secretary when Stuart joined the club his greatest challenge was to just hold on to the ground for some time because he sensed quickly the depth of political waters in the club. He knew that it was not only professional work delivery that would matter but also goodwill amongst the members of the club, particularly amongst the influential ones, which would ensure his long-term success in the club.

After joining the club, Stuart spent his initial few days in the office chamber that was part of the Superintendent's office complex but soon came up with a plan for constructing a new administrative block. He proposed to the board a plan of an administrative block in modern layout to suit the growing aspirations of golfers, that was necessary to serve the membership efficiently.

He opined that it would help in creating a good working environment and efficient workflow dynamics that would lead to high productivity of staff and thus better professional services to the members. A plan for a new administrative block building was drawn and it was proposed to build it at the spot where an old caddy shack existed. The plan was approved and the caddy shack shifted towards the course maintenance complex. Soon the new building was inaugurated having all state-of-the-art facilities to manage a golf course in the modern era. Stuart was tech-savvy, and he brought a new perspective to the management of the Club.

In the early days of his tenure, the visitors to the secretary's office were not many. They dropped in only if there was any matter that needed his personal attention. However, Stuart's servitude, and easy to approach nature encouraged members to frequent his office for seeking his personalized attention in all matters related to their membership, trifle or otherwise. This had cut short the effort of members to stand in a queue in front of the office clerks' service counters, for filling forms, paying dues or other such routine club affairs.

This also cultivated unprecedented goodwill for the new secretary in the club; soon he earned a reputation of a most likeable secretary of CGC which ensured his quick stabilization in the club and his seat appeared secured to him. But this also inculcated an attitude amongst the members where they turned over-friendly to Stuart, a difficult professional proposition and consequently his office became a casual haunt for many of them.

If CGC was the second home for its members then the Secretary's office became a drawing-room for many, particularly for the members of the Old Families. It was not only because it had a downy sofa against the side of the glass wall to lounge and look at the animated panoramic golf scene but it was a strategic eyrie. It was a comfortable spacious private space that had a large CCTV screen fed with multiple cameras and it was easy for the secretary or his acquaintances to get a quick glimpse of all the happenings in the club. From his office, it was easy to know who is having a chat with whom, and in what mood and manner, without them noticing that they are being noticed.

Therefore, members having an interest in the public affairs of the Club frequented his chamber to have a quick knowledge of the current affairs of the club. A few days' peeps from the eyrie were sufficient to give a fair understanding of who is on friendlier terms with whom and who is on the verge of a breakup. Secretary was anyway there to help with his insights to decipher the matters in detail, in case the member hailed from one of the Founding Families of the club and coaxed him for his contribution.

The office of the secretary was at a very fine location but his time was spent mostly in the Boardroom. He spent almost all his day organizing, and attending meetings with the same dozen General Committee members, although the meetings had different names assigned; Finance committee, F&B Committee, House Committee, Tournament and Handicapping Committee. Further, somebody suggested the Club needs to digitalize its operations and a new committee was born, the IT committee. Project Committees, Disciplinary Committee, and other Core Committees were formed and disbanded from time to time as per the needs and fancies of the committee members.

Stuart's day in Club typically passed convening meetings from morning till evening, getting the minutes prepared, making agendas, getting the Action Taken Reports ready and so on. Through years of experience, though he had mastered the art of gathering, the skill of synthesizing solemn excuses for all that was not done was something unique to Stuart. But when it is a routine, and nothing concludes in meetings it takes its toll.

The Club Clans

It was Saturday, the weather was fine for a good round of golf, and the course was packed with players. It was a day full of fun, golf and giggles for the club visitors but for Stuart, it was just another day! A day with back-to-back meetings. He detested meetings, but this is what he was doing all through his career in CGC. The meetings were endless in Stuart's life; Tournament Log Review Meetings, Open House Meetings, Ordinary Meetings, Extraordinary Meetings, and also the meetings with members who get into his office unannounced.

After parking his car in the lot, he walked briskly to the office block, handed over his brown brief bag to Tia, his PA and receptionist, and moved quickly straight to the boardroom for the Finance Committee meeting that was scheduled for 9.30 am. He had his quick lunch somewhere in between the Log Review Meeting of an upcoming tournament, and evening tea in the Core Committee Meeting for a project. Finally, all spent and exhausted he emerged from the boardroom ambling behind the members in the corridor who then descended down the stairs still engrossed in their never-ending discussions.

For Stuart the day-long meetings were all about extended explanations, and sometimes excuses. He was expected to explain the over expenditures in the last quarter, present the report on the course conditions, brief the committee about club's preparation for the upcoming major tournaments and present an Action Taken Report with reference to the past committee meetings. He was expected to keep all data and financial statistics ready for quick reference of the committee, mostly at the back of his mind. Members expected him to remember what all has happened in the club in the years gone by in detail, and his photogenic memory was put to test in the boardroom very often.

By the time the committee dispersed in late afternoon, Stuart was sapped up of his spirit and energy but as he pushed open the door of his office chamber, he found Mrs Green occupying all of the visitor's chairs; on one she herself was comfortable and on the other her poodle was relaxing. A portion of secretary's large desk was occupied by her handbag, a pink floral parasol, an open *Golf Glitz*, and a saucer with leftover cookie crumbs in it. An empty cup of coffee was lying on the desk and one-half empty was in her hand. It appeared as if she had been waiting for him for a long.

When Stuart stepped in, she seemed to have been concentrating on some outside objects of interest, and apparently failed to notice the door that was now ajar. Her penetrating eyes looked outside through the thick glass of her spectacles and that of the window panes. Her sight was intently fixed on Mrs Parker and Mrs Gardner on a paved walk near the practice putting green, who were into some close conversations as if in whispers. Owing to her old age Mrs Rachel was hard of hearing, but her twinkling two eyes compensated for her ears.

Further, she had been the star golfer of the club in her heydays and was one of the founding members of the Ladies Section of Capital Golf Club. But importantly she was the wife of Mr Billy Green and more importantly the member of one of the Founding Families of the club.

Founding families of the club were those whose forefathers were the primary founding members of the club, and who have done something of higher consequence for the club in its formative years. Primarily there were four founding families: the Greens, the Parkers, the Gardeners and the Flores, who were considered the founding families of the CGC, and just by tradition they commanded more respect and exercised more power, or in other words influence in the club than any other late joiners, or less mortal members of the club.

One of the highly influential founding families of the club was that of Mr Billy, his father the senior Billy was the founding member of the club and was also one who saved the club from its existential crises by providing regular funding for several years, during World War and he was able to convince few more members to contribute and keep up the club afloat while it was struggling to sustain itself. Had he not come forward to support it, the course would have gone to the hands of the government or army.

The club sustained through the war and later flourished, and so did the families who kept it afloat. Later almost all other family connections of these founding families kept connecting with the club, paying their subscription religiously irrespective of whether they played golf or not. However, in present times the four founding families command and control club functioning because they comprise a significant share of the votes in elections, which is real power in a democracy.

Many of these clans were connected by family, marriage, and businesses, sometimes even with secrets that they shared in common. This web of relations kept them glued together, especially against the other members of the club. Also, their cumulative block of votes determined the results of elections in the club, and year after year the Captain and the Presidents were either from these four families or those who were patronized by them.

In the early days of the club, however, they were decided in the pub by the father of Mr Billy with a raising of hands. In the days of senior Mr Green, nobody ever dared to go against his will, and names nominated by him were considered elected unopposed. Later the times changed, but not very much with regard to club elections because still, no one went against the will of the four founding families.

In the club, other than golf there were many struggles, one of them was the power struggle in the four families amongst themselves, and also with the new members. The domination in the new democratic club set up was by virtue of the power of votes. Earlier, the family of Greens led the club but later when membership and the voters in the club increased, the four families were forced to act more cohesively to keep the reins of club management in their hands. Nonetheless, through generations, these families somehow succeeded in controlling the club management.

Though the power politics to gain direct control of club management through the electorate was quite obvious amongst the four families, but a delicate balance always existed. They competed freely with each other but when their dominance was challenged by an outsider, they came together to keep others out of the competition using the tools of rules and regulations and using the shield of bylaws and articles of the constitution.

The other lot of the members, therefore either electorally aligned with one of the four families and became a part of a lobby, or just cared only about playing golf, which was in any way in the interest of the four families. These four families sometimes came together in a set of two each and made two lobbies or one joined hands with the other and resulted in three lobbies and so on, however, there never existed a new front of the new members who could challenge the old-clans despite having their vote in the club.

These families commanded influence to affect any of the decisions of the board or the boardroom because even if they were not on the seat, they still had their reps in the committee. These families also had the favour of most of the new joiners too, because they became members only with the support and favours of these four families, therefore their loyalties always lay with one of the families of the founding families.

Since the tradition of golf began in the capital, the four families drew power from the old-time traditional support and the foundational obligation that members felt for them. It mostly made people agree to their commands for their decisions were always perceived to be in the interest of the club and for the good of the game.

Initially, it was more of an informal world, but steadily democracy changed the power dynamics, where power came from secret votes rather than the raising of hands; still, the stronghold of the founding families continued in the form of soft power, which was more gripping and elegant than the stronghold approach. Now they necessarily didn't have to work hard to push or prompt actions, for the soft power is more effective and cleaner to operate within a democratic dispensation.

In present times these families are often referred to as resourceful families rather than powerful, therefore, still they managed to command the fealty of most members to themselves. The families seemed to have already mastered the art of influencing the members in a modern set-up and retaining their allegiance.

The office of the secretary though was vested with all the necessary powers to run the club professionally, but in practice, the secretary was bound to follow the committee which always was constituted largely by the members of the founding families, year after year. So, in effect, the secretary was obliged to obey these families of the club respectfully.

When Stuart joined CGC more than a decade ago, he realized that to play a long inning in this club he needed to be in the good books of old families, gaining their favours was necessary for his survival in the club. Sensing this, he quickly opened his heart and office to the founding family members, sometimes silently ignoring the common rules of the club, ensuring convenience to his actual masters in the club. It certainly has paid back; it was already now more than a decade and he still held the coveted seat of secretary of the CGC.

However, favours are exchanged not given, and so over the years, his geniality got him into a situation where he struggled to have moments of privacy, even in his own office because it was mostly occupied by someone or the other. Today it was Mrs Green who was there enjoying the verdant panorama through the window of the secretary's office.

'Hello, madam,' Stuart greeted Mrs Rachel, drawing her attention.

Turning her head towards the door, she made a quick reciprocation, 'Hi... Hi, Stuart!'

'I am sorry, it appears you have been waiting for me for too long,' said Stuart, with a smile, stretched on his face.

'Not too long, Stuart. You have a very kind lady at the reception, who took care of me perfectly, even when you were not in the office.'

'Certainly, she is a great help to me and our members too,' said Stuart. 'I am aware of your grandson's dependent card, it's all prepared and was ready for dispatch today. Did Tia hand over the card to you?'

'She did and told me that you were in a meeting, but I thought when I am here, why not say a little "Hi" to you.'

'So nice of you, madam, it has been a long time since you've been seen in the club?'

'I was in London this summer, and also moved to Edinburgh for a few days to see Bubbles, close to her, Jas is also there at the university'.

'Oh, that's good. How is she doing there? The club misses its talented golfer dearly. When is she finishing college?'

'She is in her last semester in college and will be back in the next few months.'

Stuart was a busy man; his whole day was spent meeting people either in the boardroom or in his own office with people who came with an appointment or with those who had the privilege of getting in unannounced. In any case, he rarely had a chance to sit and relax in silence even in his own office. It was already late afternoon and he was just thinking of somehow escaping Mrs Green, and then on his intercom, Tia informed him about an arrival of a team of surveyors and the superintendent from DLGR who were in waiting to see him.

He consented to let them in and asked Tia to pass a message to Golf Operations for organizing a six-seater golf cart for having a round of the golf course with the guests. Putting down the phone piece, he politely informed Mrs Green about his next engagement with an important delegation. The guests were admitted in soon, and seeing more people pouring in, Mrs Green quickly wrapped herself up and her belongings, and left the chamber bidding a quick bye to the secretary.

The guests were made comfortable following a few courtesy handshakes. Secretary then rang Olie to join him for the course tour with the guests. Shortly, the team of surveyors and Stuart were seen descending the stairs and boarding a six-seater golf cart, Olie was already there on the steering wheel. They cruised through the course and came to a stop at the 18th green, the surveyors began setting up their survey station near the green.

A fourball that approached the green 18th to putt, asked the secretary, 'What is going on?'. In a low, dull voice he responded, 'The measurement of 18th green disputed land area, the survey is being done as per the court's order. The date for the final verdict is approaching.'

The golfer asked, 'Are we really going to lose this green to DLGR?'

In a stifled voice, the secretary uttered, 'The Core Committee is meeting Bobby shortly, and hopefully matters would be resolved soon in our favour.'

At the 18th green, Stuart and Olie stood silently striving to hide expressions of defeat and dullness as the members from the terrace of the clubhouse bar watched the team and its setup of measuring tools. In a round straw hat, an old man was focusing intently on the happenings at the 18th green. The moment Stuart and Olie realized his presence at the terrace, with a slight bow they immediately conveyed their deferential respect in distance to the old man. The bow was reciprocated with a gentle nod.

The old man pulled out his phone and pressed a few keys. Next moment Stuart's phone pinged with an SMS reading: What's on? Brief me, when done. Stuart immediately responded, 'Sure, Uncle Woodie.'

Stuart, however, didn't wait for the survey team to finish their tasks, instead, he asked Olie to stick with them and he left the 18th green and performed the distance from the green to the Terrace Bar with quick steps and ascended the stairs. Reaching the door of the bar, he slowed his steps and calmed his breath before accosting Uncle Woodie who was seated in the corner of the Terrace Bar, at his usual front corner table facing the finishing hole of the game.

He was intently observing the performances at his favourite theatre, the 18th green. After having a sip from an old-fashioned glass, he placed the cut-crystal diamante tumbler on the table. A soft silvery logo of CGC etched on its surface shined against its golden content giving a golden hue to the table with dim overhead lamps. He pulled a pack of Robusta from his coat pocket, picked a stick neatly and placed it in between his lips, and before he could reach for a lighter in his pocket, a waiter standing nearby quickly sprang in, lit his cigar with a lighter, and withdrew with equal quickness.

Though it appeared windy and chilly outside, the inner ambience of the glass-walled bar was cosy and comfortable. As dusk began to gather outside, the crowd began to build inside the bar. In the fireplace, a cheerful fire burnt and all the seatings around the hearth were occupied one after the other. The kindling was added and the fire stoked, the happy faces shone brightly near the hearth, and people exchanged season's greetings, the air was festive.

The overhead flood lights on the 18th green lit up with a flicker, drawing the attention of the Oldest Golfer who was lost silently in his inner merriments of good old memories of the past. Through the glass curtain wall, he saw a group putting on the 18th green, the fog had begun to build as was visible in the diffused light of the halogen bulbs on the masts. Far in the foggy fairway, a fourball was also seen standing, possibly the last one, waiting for the green to clear.

The Oldest Golfer drew a dreg from his glass, followed by a pull from his cigar. In the evening air of the still corner of the bar as the rings of smoke began to rise into roundelays, the old man receded into a reverie; remembering and reminiscing the pleasant past. It was the 18th green where he had held up many cups and clarets in his heydays. He had seen a lot of golf, game and a grind of manly emotions culminating at the 18th green.

Uncle Woodie as he was called by everyone in the club was one of the oldest members of the club. Some also called him the 'Oldest Golfer' because although he doesn't go into the course anymore, still he putts routinely on the practice putting green, every evening, before ascending to the terrace for his evening drinks.

Not only in the club but also in the golfing circles of the capital he was regarded very highly. He dedicated his life to the love of the game whatever was left to him after serving in the National Army.

In his younger days, he was known as one of the finest golfers in the country and in later years as a designer and architect of some of the finest golf courses that still exist in the country as a testament to his understanding of the game and his passion for the sport. He was also one of the first greenkeepers of the country.

In the relaying and modification of CGC, Uncle Woodie played a pivotal role, and his inclination toward the old-school golf design philosophy was obvious in his work in the course. During his early days while on one of his golfing visits to England, he happened to meet Dr Alister Mackenzie and since then had been a fan of his philosophy of course architecture and greenkeeping. It is believed that while relaying the course of CGC he was in correspondence with Dr Mackenzie through the exchange of letters and the course reflects a typical Mackenzie mindset, where every hole is enjoyable for every player irrespective of his playing skills.

The previous committees made several attempts to reconstruct the golf course with drastic design changes to meet the modern requirements of international golf, but Uncle Woodie single-handedly thwarted all such attempts of tinkering with the classic golf course layout for all these years.

He often said, don't transform the existing classic courses completely, they are the heritage golf courses which have their own old charm, if need be, look for making new courses with modern designs. The earth anyway needs more golf courses for they are the peace-providing abodes to city dwellers who mostly are bogged down in the buzz of high-decibel city life.

Uncle Woodie had developed many courses not only for the army but also had his hands in several other classic courses in the country. He was revered not only as an army veteran but also as a celebrity golfer of the past, a veteran golf architect and as a pioneer greenkeeper of the country. Other than all this he has a rich family legacy as he hails from one of the noble lineages of the country.

Stuart walked to the table where Uncle Woodie was seated, and after a courteous salutation took a seat at a gesture from the veteran. He then explained in detail about the court case and the ongoing progress pertaining to it, including the measurement survey that was going on in front of them on the court's order as they saw the team at work from the terrace.

From the cigar tucked in his mouth, he pulled a puff, following which it hung in his hand for some time, and with sealed lips, listened silently to what all was recited to him. He then let out the smoke that swirled in his mouth for all this while, and questioned, 'What time will the committee leave for his club?'

'At 11 am, Sir.'

'Has Bobby confirmed his availability for tomorrow's core committee meeting at his club?'

'His PA has not yet confirmed his availability, but his VP would be there for discussions.'

'Convey a message to him, that I will be accompanying the core committee tomorrow and would like to see him.'

'Sure, Sir. Will do.'

Secretary then took leave paying his obeisance respectfully to Uncle Woodie and stepped down the terrace. However, it was already late evening so instead of going back to his office, he moved straight to the parking lot. Finally, he was off for the day.

PART 2

The Rival Club

The next morning, at 11 am the core committee of CGC and Uncle Woodie left for Divine Luxury Golf Resort. They drove across the road took a U-turn from a nearby roundabout, and within a few minutes, the delegation was at the doors of DLGR, the entrance of one of the finest and grandest golf properties in the world.

The car carrying the distinguished delegation stopped briefly for a formal security check at the entrance of the club. Uncle Woodie observed the grandeur of the gate and for a seasoned eye, a glimpse of the magnificence of the main entrance was enough to foresee the show behind the gates. The consequences of hurt self-esteem are often big for sure, but this time they appeared impressive too.

A man can go to great lengths to protect his honour, certainly, but to avenge his dented honour, it appears he could go a bit beyond that length. The testament was right there in the form of DLGR. The golf course that grew from grounds in the last couple of years now rivals the ancient club from the front. Not because it stands face to face right across the road in front of the Capital Golf Club, but because its genesis has its roots in rivalry, clash of conceits, and conflict of manly egos!

The rivalry between the ancient CGC and the modern DLGR was no more subtle now, it had turned stark and straight. Since its inception, the National Open has been held at CGC, the original home of the most reputed golf tournament in the country. But now it has drifted across the road on the pretext of better course conditions and high-end facilities for international golfers, organizers and visiting spectators.

There were rumours that the tournament went to DLGR completely, however after some closed-room negotiations with the tour, the format of the tournament was modified to a multi-course event. The first two days were scheduled to be played at DLGR and the last two days at CGC.

Several insiders claimed in hushed voices that this was done just to respect the long relationship that the tournament had with CGC. Those who could read between the lines knew that the charm of CGC was steadily thinning out. In the eyes of the golfers and the tour, not everything was good at CGC, anymore; even if it was assumed to be so, it certainly was better across the road.

CGC dominated the turf of the capital for more than a century, for there was no one to dispute the dominance of the big old club. Few new golf courses did come up in the past decades but none had the scale, resources and intentions to challenge the grandeur that CGC commanded. Be it an individual or an institution, achieving the title of *Numero Uno* is not that big a deal but defending it, is.

Even if there exists no imminent rival to challenge the status quo, still, time, though invisible, is a coactive rival. If one fails to keep up a lead with time, sooner or later the time topples the topper for sure. It was not that CGC hasn't changed or improved with time but it didn't change enough, and certainly not enough to remain on top in the modern competitive era of golf.

The past century was a century of change. The changes were quick and palpable in every aspect of our lifestyle, especially in the recent few decades. The latest innovations have been quick disruptors of our good old pace of living. There has been inevitable and immense meddling of technology in our day-to-day living, it changed the way we interact not only with each other but also with our environment, things, and nature.

The game of golf also evolved with time, though it is still played with sticks and balls, and the hole remains the same where eventually a ball sinks, but the ball has changed from featherie, to gutty to rubber core; the clubs from Woods to Irons to Graphite and Titanium. The game too changed, if not in spirit than at least how it is played and presented.

A few decades ago, the drives in golf seldom touched 300 yards but today it's an achievable feat by many pros. The courses which were wrapped within 7000 yards often in yesteryears are now stretched out beyond that limit to meet modern expectations. Grasses that were commonly native and natural have steadily been replaced with hybrid dwarfs, to modern ultradwarfs.

The mowers have gone robotic and manless, irrigation automated, spraying computerized and the soil signals its requirements straight to the superintendent through subsoil sensors. Golf maintenance has become more precise, more sophisticated and golf operation has gone intensively technology-driven. Even the Rules of Golf changed to suit the expectations of modern golf and golfers. All in all, the game of golf has transformed drastically, the perception about it also has changed, it has become more melodramatic, and more moneyed!

Earlier golfing tracks were twined intricately with landscapes of a locality, and almost everybody had access to the verdant nature and its game. However, since the time land began appreciating in value, and encroachments on the boundless golf properties became recurrent, the continuum of a golf course with its surroundings got broken by newly erected boundary walls. Whatever may the reason be, but most modern golf courses are now walled and gated to keep the trespassers at bay. Most golf courses now exist in confinements, and consequently have receded away from the reach of the common man, to whom it actually belonged.

Originally the game was founded by the masses, the aristocracy arrived later in the arena. Nevertheless, the golfing world even today looks divided in this regard, a part of it still strives hard to make it a sport of the masses again, while a section of the high society which drew it up from its original grounds and now dominates the game appear determined to keep it as the game of the rich and famous. They continuously invent means and methods to keep it exclusive, beyond the easy reach of the masses.

Originally, golf was played on sandy links where grass grew naturally, sheep mowed it at no cost, and passionate golfers just needed to pick a stick and a ball to begin with their round. But today playing the game is an expensive affair, a hobby that can be pursued mostly by the man of means. Modern golf is about slick surfaces, and sophisticated machinery to maintain them, and golfers need an expensive range of playing paraphernalia to perform their complete golfing rites.

Nowadays in a short span of time, golfing assets and materials are rendered outdated, and continuous investment in the upgrade of golfing facilities has become a norm; It is a race against time that very few could afford to run.

Further, every year prominent golf publications release their golf course rankings, and some agencies associated with the game of golf even come up to give away awards based on the criteria known best to them. In this fast-paced technology-driven golfing environment remaining on top is a task in itself, not only for golfers but for the golf courses too.

Bobby, however, believed that 'traditions too have a beginning'. He was confident that his dream project, DLGR, was all set to start a tradition, a tradition of luxury golf living. To be the top and the most exclusive golf club in the world. Surprisingly, within its few years of birth, DLGR is now the most talked-about golf course in the world.

The course has caused enough flaunt and flutter owing to the money that has gone down in creating the masterpiece. Bobby proclaimed his commitment to work seriously for the game with his very first project in the capital. He was ready not only to run but also to win the race of golf-centric real estate business in the country.

Money was a matter of least concern at DLGR because the owner not only had begun to hit long drives in his own exclusive golf course but also had been hitting the headlines and front pages of the *Times* and *Forbes*.

Bobby with his interests in multinational businesses and stakes in steel, mining and real estate has already begun challenging the richest and wealthiest of the world. Bobby's business empire was crossing borders with leaps and bounds. Leave aside Tom, Dick, and Harries of golf; Bobby was there on the turf now to challenge other Bobs and Bobbies of the golfing world and their wealthy clubs!

Bobby seemed to have taken the rivalry and his golf course pretty seriously. It appears as if he was now daring to challenge even the august land of golf and masters of the golf tournaments. He ensured that his greens were the greenest in the world; the sand in the bunkers the whitest and the water in its lakes the bluest, no matter what it took to create and maintain such features. There were rumours in golfing circles that he was organizing the funds and resources to bring down the best players of the world to his course. Apparently, a towel was already thrown and the masters of the game felt shaken by the winds of change that rose from the other end of the golfing world.

DLGR was Bobby's dream project; it was there to make a statement of grandeur and luxury. It was an invitation for the world's wealthy to experience the richness of golf and living, both together. Those who had the means to afford the coveted pass into the world of Bobby's imagination often described it as fantasy land. The awe-inspiring stories of the grandeur behind the gates of DLGR sometimes appeared unbelievable; a description from the fables of fantasies.

The entry to the DLGR was guarded by armed security men in uniform and with a massive wrought iron entrance gate. The colossal gate was crafted with patterns of vines, roses, crowns and scrolls of spades and hearts in metal; it evoked grandeur and regality. The gate rose mighty high, in extravagance, with its spikes and finials topped with golden *fleur-de-lis*.

For the guests, after the security checks, the automated gates slid open smoothly opening up into an awe-inspiring wide and long driveway. A mile or a two long approach driveway, lined on both sides with thickly crowned tall trees in the distance. The metaled road that ran in the centre was kerbed on its sides and edged neatly with manicured plant hedges. A green carpet of velvety grass also ran all along the driveway on both sides as a long lawn with spills of colourful flowers in pockets, elegantly filling the grounds between the driveway hedge and the dark green tree line.

The driveway eventually circled around a huge white-winged female figurine, carved in white marble, the roundabout was landscaped with exotic plants, elegant light heads and a fountain flowing dramatically within the circle. At the circle, the driveway splits into two service ways, one leading to the world's most premium golf community residences and the other to the iconic clubhouse of one of the most highly rated modern golf courses of the world.

The delegation of CGC reached the clubhouse of the DLGR, and the car carrying them stopped at its porch, which was grand and expansive. When the guests entered the grand and opulent lobby, they were awestruck by the sheer scale of the building compared to the one that they have at CGC and call their clubhouse. Though a clubhouse has nothing much to do with the golf course per se, still, it not only states the vision of the owners for the place and foretells what to expect while on the property but also sets the mood for a game.

In a golf course, the clubhouse holds a unique place though its original purpose was to house golfers and their equipment, with time the clubhouse acquired other dimensions as well. Every golf course has a unique clubhouse which often reflects the tradition and vision of the club owners and the people promoting such facilities, most often they become the signature structures of the club. Modern clubhouses are designed to have a unique look and they evoke a peculiar sensibility to them, after all, they are exceptional spaces and are expected to surprise and impress visitors.

Clubhouses are bespoke buildings, tailored to suit the surroundings and sensibilities of the owners of the property. They are often created taking cues from the culture and class that it would be housing. The place is of importance to the residents and owners of these golfing properties, for it gives a sense of pride to them and conveys their long-cherished collective culture to the outside world.

However, the measure of the magnificence of a particular clubhouse is judged mostly against its rivals in the vicinity. In the case of Bobby's clubhouse, the sense of one-upmanship naturally persisted in the form of heightened pride about the place. It was adorned fittingly with a ribbon of rivalry that added an additional charm to his conquest over the courses and their clubhouses not only in the vicinity but across the continents.

At DLGR, the design of the clubhouse was modern yet imposing. It boldly made the statement that there the game was big! It could have been mistaken easily for a magnificent palace of the present day. It was a result of exceptional architecture and high-end interior design, with a well-thought consideration of the surroundings and the owners' objective behind the creation of such an exclusive piece of property. It resonated aptly with the one-upmanship of its owner, with its incredible style and architecture that tied subtly with the measured nuances, and thought-out design performances. It was a monument made for ages to come, the building was built with timeless materials, colours and contours that rendered it an exceptional guest experience.

At the clubhouse, a six-seater golf cart was waiting for the core committee. The members alighted on the silent vehicle which conveyed them quickly to the administrative complex of the DLGR. The members of the committee were conducted to the Boardroom of the DLGR with all honour by the staff at the office entrance. The delegates from CGC took their seats in the boardroom of DLGR as the GM facilitated them to get comfortable. In a few minutes, the Vice-President of the DLGR also appeared, and the meeting began but Bobby was missing from the boardroom.

Bobby was known to the world not only as a lawyer, and a parliamentarian but also as a business magnet. He was a personality, known very well in the upper circles of society as the one who gambits casually. When no one dared, his father put forth his feet in dealing with the government and began constructing the new city several decades ago.

Even in the present day, probably half of the buildings in the capital have been erected with the concrete churned out from his factories. The company has grown not only into a real estate giant in the world but also has stakes in major sunshine sectors of the world economy.

Many of his peers who lost against him on one or other occasions, often described him as a gamester with tongue-in-cheeks. But he flaunts his gamesmanship as one-upmanship and takes pride in what he has achieved for himself and the nation. He often says that though he has not ruled the nation, he has built the capital from where the nation is ruled. He proudly proclaims that his family had stood for the nation when it needed the most, putting all their wealth at stake during the wars.

Bobby fought multiple battles all through his life, but never lost, never gave up, and never surrendered in his long career in business and politics. He cherished rivalries and believed that those who are incapable of handling competition call it a rivalry. He says competition pleases him and winning pleases him even more. Therefore, he ensures that he always wins, no matter what it takes to do so.

After a long-stretched discussion in the boardroom of DLGR, it appeared that they were in no mood to compromise on the 18th green, finally, Uncle Woodie picked up his qwerty phone and sent a text: *r u comin? I am waiting to see u!* Uncle Woodie knew that Bobby would not defer his direct message and in the next few minutes, Bobby entered the room, exchanged courtesy greetings, and shook hands with the guests, eventually seating himself.

Uncle Woodie said, 'Bobby, CGC is a national heritage of golf in the country and your father had been instrumental in developing the city, he had a vision of an international city for the capital. The golf course was one key element in the design of the new city and your father's vision of the grand capital city always had a place for CGC. I don't understand why you are adamant about tinkering with the heritage of the city'.

Sensing Uncle Woodie's attempt to give it an emotional spin, Bobby immediately interrupted his speech and said, 'I definitely agree with you Uncle, and we are committed to making the capital city one of the best cities in the world. I am working on the vision of my late father and am committed to developing the finest residences in the city. However, it is not me alone to have a say on 18th green, actually, residents of the DLGR community collectively have its ownership. Because when the community was being developed and sold, that parcel of land was shown to the clients as a part of DLGR golf city. We have now developed all the areas as per our committed plan, the 18th green area that is presently being occupied by CGC, only remains. Still, Uncle Woodie, we would try convincing the residents of the DLGR Golf City if they could consider forfeiting that land to CGC. We are bound by the commitment to the city owners, to whom we had sold properties with the design layout of DLGR course that stretched across the road'.

The meeting concluded only with informal assurances but without a firm commitment from Bobby, which was as good as saying 'no'. However, though Bobby was brash in his routine attitude he remained calm and composed all through his dealing with Uncle Woodie in the boardroom. Uncle Woodie observed that Bobby whispered some silent words to his GM. The General Manager then offered the guests to drop them at the Club House where their car was parked.

The GM took a different route to the Club House than the short one which they followed while coming, which avoided the golf course. While on their retreat, cruising from one hole to the other, the committee members appreciated the sheer beauty and magnificence of the course as they detoured through the golf course. DLGR is known for its remarkable palatial clubhouse, sumptuous sprawls of the lavish golf community, and the world's best amenities designed and conceptualized by professionals extraordinaire.

However, the centric beauty around which all these luxe and lavish indulgences were woven was the sprawling championship golf course that is one of its kind, presented immaculately in a picture-perfect form, round the year.

The course was designed on the theme of different climatic zones of the world. Each hole was a unique locale in itself. You start from a Scandinavian feel on the first hole, pass through the desert holes and finish at the island green of the 18th. Here the island could drift so the course played different yardage each day. All this magic has been made possible by investing in the customized infrastructure and the latest technology that went behind the scenes to maintain this dreamland image of the golf course.

The golf cart cruised through the course and the members were immersed in the overwhelming beauty of the course. The committee couldn't initially understand the actual intent of a long detour through the course. However, when they crossed the 18th hole, they saw a bright new plaque with an arrow pointing toward the road, with a caption: This is a temporary green in play, the main green is across the road and will be open for play shortly.

The intent was now obvious. The core group might have missed the intent of the detour but Uncle Woodie, who read the gestures of Mr Bobby understood that it was on purpose. The weird plaque pronounced clearly that Bobby had no intent and was in no mood to forfeit his claim to the 18th green of CGC, irrespective of whatever he said in the meeting.

Bobby's notoriety for settling scores with noise was known very well, but here he employed a silent pointer that directed the ridicule subtly across the road, to the CGC. The plaque was placed on purpose, which aroused curiosity in golfers who finish their final hole and get into the Clubhouse with a topic to discuss in the way they choose.

The meeting was anyway inconclusive, and the committee members boarded their car to get back to their club carrying a feeling of failure in their hearts. Uncle Woodie, however, was not prepared to give up hope, he felt duty-bound to find a way out to salvage the 18th green. Whenever the club landed in any crisis in the past, some or other members from the founding families came forward to rescue it. Now, it was Uncle Woodie's turn for he was not only the oldest member but also hailed from the founding families of the club, if he could not save the green, who else would?

It was now not only about a stretch of land, but about the reputation of the club in general and that of the founding families of the club in particular. Uncle Woodie decided to take charge of the crisis into his own hands before it gets too late. There was no way now he could leave the matters to the hands of the club management committee or the secretary. Uncle Woodie dialled an international number.

The voice responded, 'Hello, Uncle Woodie'.

'Hi Bubbles, how are you, how is everything there in Edinburgh?'

'All good, Uncle.'

'Well, Bubbles, I had a meeting with Bobby today, as expected he appears adamant on his claim for 18th green, we need to do something to make him understand. Nobody knows him and his weaknesses better than you, I think you could make him bend. It is time to act, or else it would be too late.'

Bubbles heard him patiently and then said, 'I am anyway going to see Jas this weekend and would play a round of golf at the Old Course. Also, there I would meet Joy, Bob's son, who also is reading there with Jas at the university. He is an understanding boy and might help to rein in Bob. Don't you worry Uncle, I will see how to handle it.'

Bobby, Billy, and Bubbles were friends since school and this continued till their college. However, after college, as youngsters, they had their choices to make and so they walked their own ways in life.

Eventually, the roads they travelled led them to different locations, separating them not only in person but in thinking too. Uncle Woodie, however, knew that once friends are always friends, especially the tender relations of childhood are not easily buried, they are often respected even by the stone-hearted. Uncle Woodie was sure that if Bobby would hear somebody, then she is none other than Bubbles.

The Game of Love

At the Scottish seaside, it was a Saturday afternoon of early summer. The sun soared, though sluggishly at a snail's pace. However, the haar that hung over the skies since morning began to thin out. The sprinkle of sunshine gently uncovered the sandy links that lay hidden under a shroud of a thick mist since morning. The sun gained more vigour, and the fog dissipated leaving the links, but it remained reluctantly on the adjoining waters. The fog rather got intense over the ocean, mystically merging the sea and sky as one on the watery horizon, as if in agitation.

Apparently, the sun was more biased to the sands than to the sea, the afternoon got crispier with the brightening of the sun on the sandy links but the sea was all turbid. The landscape was split into contrasting scenes side by side; vivid bright links with glistening greens on one side and an adjoining bleak grey sea with heaps of fog.

Over the old course, the weekend winds that rose from coastal waters were wet and cold but were unusually calm. The sunshine was soft and comforted golfers, the warmth in the ambience was obvious from a build-up of players at the practice putting green, where a group gathered for a warm-up putting. Further, as soon as the visibility improved a bit, and it was enough to trace the trajectory of the tee shot the golfers began to beeline at the first tee. They were ready for a round of golf, now the players were in good humour.

Aiming for the fairway of the silky green course, they teed, and hit their first shots, at the success of their first stroke the smiles on their faces widened making them more cheerful. Golfers are a hopeful lot; it takes very little to keep their spirits high. They never expect a perfect world to perform and play their best game. Particularly at the first tee, they could be excited, anxious, or restless but are seldom passive.

Jas, whose tee-off was scheduled in the next few minutes with her aunt, Bubbles, however, looked dull and dreary. She was seated next to the starter's hut, clasping a cup of coffee, watching intently the tempestuous mass of mist hovering over the sea, in silence. She gazed at the rolling sea fog with unblinking eyes as if trying to discern the sea and sky from the continuum that it created.

At the same time, the day appeared bright and dull, depending on which side one looked, however, while waiting for the arrival of her aunt, Jas seemed to have been lost in her own thoughts. Her face was mirroring moods ranging from confusion to undecidedness, her heart clouded with self-doubts. But surely, she was neither worried about her game nor was overwhelmed by nature's fickleness. Irrespective of weather conditions a weekend round was a norm for her since the time she landed in the tiny town of the Scottish seaside to pursue her studies and the game of golf.

In spite of all the academic engagements at university, as a disciplined student, she managed her studies during the week and dedicated her weekend to pursuing her passion for golf. She had played all the seven courses of the golfing town in rotation to keep perfecting her skills not only in different weathers but in different terrain as well.

Jas has just completed her university and was overstaying a few more days in the town, maybe to play and practise the courses there a few more times. However, even while at the university, she followed a playing discipline too for she was to turn pro in the upcoming golf season.

While she was deep in her thoughts, Bubbles, her aunt, parked her car in the lot adjoining the golf course and approached the starter's hut with quick steps to play a scheduled round of golf with her beloved niece after a long time. However, when she saw Jas musing in a reverie, she called her name.

'Hey, Jas, where are you lost? What are you searching for in the distant grey sea? Get ready, babe! I am here, it's time to win the greens!'.

Jas woke up with a jerk of the head, and an affected animation appeared on her face quickly as she attempted to behave like a golfer.

Quickly, she responded, 'Oh, dear aunt, you are already here! It was the floating fog on the sea that caught my sight and I missed to notice you coming.'

'That's fine! But don't get drifted with it, let's walk to the tee, it's almost time to tee off.'

Jas and her aunt reached the first tee, and as a mark of courtesy from her niece, Aunt Bubbles had the honour on the tee! She pierced the turf of the teeing ground with a wooden tee and placed a new golf ball delicately on its receptacle. While preparing to take her stance for her first shot, she said, 'Playing this course is always fun, every time one plays it. Jas, good you called me up for the game. It's been a long time since we played together.'

'Indeed, it is a golfing paradise, aunt', said Jas in agreement.

Opening up after a few practice swings, Bubbles hit a fine shot splitting the fairway from the centre, like a seasoned champion of the game she hit the drive long and straight.

Appreciating the perfect shot of her aunt, Jas moved forward to tee up her ball. She was already out of focus in her thoughts and the fine shot from her aunt further set a kind of benchmark of performance, a challenge that ought to be pursued. She got a bit uneasy at this but tried her best to keep herself composed. After a practice swing, she hit the ball launching it perfectly from the cusp of the tee. The ball rose up fine but, in the distance, it began to draw slightly to the left. Still, it landed in the fairway avoiding rough by a few yards, after all, she was a prospective champion and was not expected to lose nerves and her ball to the rough so easily.

Jas acted unruffled, but nothing escaped Aunt Bubbles' eyes. She had already noted a furrow that formed briefly on her niece's forehead which she hid quickly under her tilted hat. It was not due to an odd aberration in her near-perfect shot, but was the reflection of her perturbed self. She saw the turbulence in her eyes, clearly.

Aunt Bubbles already had got the wind of turmoil in her niece's relations with Joy; her childhood friend, and long-time golf buddy. On a phone call, Jas had already conveyed to her that Joy was in some kind of family trouble and being a friend, it was hard for her to see him sinking. Observing the tone and tenor of her voice, Bubbles had sensed on that very day that the concern of Jas for Joy was more than that of a friend to an other.

Today, Bubbles, herself perceived the pent-up emotions of a heavy heart on seeing her niece. Jas was in desperate need of venting out the build-up for her own good and she was surely looking for someone to share her heart with. Probably that was the reason why she called her aunt to visit and play a round of golf with her.

Jas was unable to figure out where to begin, but everybody has their own unique tells. These patterns of behaviour might be missed by strangers but aunt Bubbles knew her niece very well. Also, she was a seasoned player of the game and knew that most often a bad game from a good player is a reflection of a turbulent mind. She was mostly spot-on in deducing exactly what is going on in the mind and heart of a player on the field. Bubbles was deft in picking such subtle signs of behaviour even of her fellow players, then how could she not read Jas, who grew in front of her eyes.

She herself took a lead to help her niece in the game of emotions, as she did help her in the game of golf on several occasions. Since the time Jas had started playing on the course, Bubbles was her first mentor who instilled in her how to deal with the game especially when the field is not in her favour. This time the game was a bit different, but games are games after all.

'Where is your friend, Joy?' said Bubbles. 'Last week, on the phone you said you have already finished college, and both of you would fly back home together, is it not! Then, suddenly what made you overstay and call me for a round of golf. I could see you are doing fine on the course, but is everything else alright, off the course?'

Jas began her walk with Bubbles from the first tee towards the fairway, having enough questions to answer till they parted to attend their golf balls in the fairway. Jas began with the second question first, the easiest one.

'All good, aunt,' responded Jas. 'Everything is fine, I overstayed this week to play a few more rounds of golf before returning home. Joy got engaged in his personal affairs as I mentioned.'

'But you had said he received a call from his father to see the girl, didn't you?'

'Yes.'

'Then, it is not Joy's personal affair or his choice, his father is imposing his decision on him, did Joy choose the girl?'

'Yes, ... No', said Jas, answering in a perplexed state of mind.

'I knew, Bobby will not change!' She muttered to herself. 'But how can he impose his decisions on a young boy, just because he is his son.'

Meanwhile, Jas' mind was busy mining the right words to start and share her own story which too was all about Joy.

As they walked a few steps together, instead of answering any further or either starting her own story, she split from her aunt a little quickly taking a sinistral side on the pretext of seeking her ball. She reached the left edge of the fairway, took her stance, addressed the ball that lay in a decent lie, and with a full swing made a clean stroke driving it towards the pin. The ball took off gaining a fair loft as if it would chase the green but before it could reach there it dipped and came to rest a few yards short of it on the margin of a greenside bunker. Bubbles on the other hand repeated her performance and led her ball straight on the green, a putt away from the pin.

Though Jas had a choice to join the walk to the green with her aunt, she continued on her walk to the greens solo keeping a distance from her aunt, probably buying more time to adjust her thoughts and frame the script more appropriately in her mind before beginning with the story. Jas made a perfect recovery shot from the thick grass of the bunker brow to a foot of the pin and then putted for a par.

To this performance, Bubbles uttered, 'What a fine recovery shot! Champions may not be perfect with every shot of their game, but all of them are necessarily good at recovering, I could certainly see that in you!'

Following this Bubbles made a gentle stroke on her ball that lay about ten yards away but with a break of green in between, the ball rolled, curved from the break but overshot the pin from the edge of the cup by a yard. She made her second putting stroke, and while picking up her ball from the hole for par said, 'In golf and in life, with every shot, we run the risk of overshooting, but equally it holds the possibility of turning out to be the recovery shot, the outcome is not in our hands but as a player, making a stroke anyway is our responsibility.'

'Certainly, aunt. I learnt that from you to keep the nerves in control when the game is not in our favour and wait for the right moment to recover', responded Jas.

While walking towards the 2nd tee, Bubbles, again brought back Joy in their conversation and said, 'What's the name of the lady you mentioned the other day on phone?'

'Liza', she answered.

'Did Joy ever shared his heart with you, I mean does he have anybody in mind whom he wishes to be his life partner? You are his best friend and close companion. Did you ask him, ever, who he has in his heart?'

'No, I never did.'

'I wonder, how could he miss a charming girl like you who was always close to him for all these years,' said Bubbles, in a teasing tone as if she was sure that both of them were made for each other.

Jas now knew not how to respond to it, with a smile or seriousness, but had no reason to avoid the discussion anymore, and with a mix of diffidence and anxiety on her face, she started sharing the stories of the time which they spent together in the small university town, and then how suddenly after a phone call from his father he got restless and rebelliously self-destructive.

The story of Jas and Joy, however, had its beginning not in the small Scottish town but in a big capital city, where they both grew up together as a kid, attended the same school, were in the same class, and played the same game, the game of golf. They were together in school, in golf course, and in each other's talks and thoughts. Growing up as friends they had passed several years and grades in school, but by the time they were about to pass high school, they felt that they didn't want to part. They found it difficult to stay away from each other and so they decided to go to the same college, so as to continue with their togetherness. Though, neither had ever acknowledged to the other that their friendship has grown to a stronger emotion which they found difficult to name but they always had the feeling of being together forever!

Jas found it hard to figure out when it all began but all she remembers is that she liked the game of golf and liked it more when Joy was with her. Somehow the golf course turned out to be a ground, where not only Jas' swing matured but also the tender emotions of love thrived in her heart, escaping her notice. Jas and Joy often spent long days repeating the 18 holes mostly not sure whether they did so to stay together or for the love of the game.

Though they have not acknowledged their love for each other yet they acknowledged to each other that their common love is golf. So they thought of pursuing this love on the oldest links and decided to pursue their college studies at one of the oldest universities in Scotland situated in a quaint little town with passionate lovers of the game. They both landed at the university that offered not only studies but also the opportunity to enhance their golfing skills by practising them on several links with which the university is flanked, this decision to choose this unique university was heartily appreciated by the golfing families of both Jas and Joy.

Jas came from a family of golfing champions, since her childhood she had been visiting Capital Golf Club with her grandparents and then with her parents not only to play but for various other activities as Mr Billy Green was mostly found at the golf course and same was the case with her mother Mrs Rachel Green when they were at the peak of their golfing career winning trophies every now and then.

Joy, on the other hand, came from a golfing business family, as his father played golf but for him, business was always the priority. For him, golf has always been a tool for business expansion. For him it was merely a game and nothing more, there is no point in dedicating a life to excelling in the game. It is more useful as a long walk where one has a good opportunity to network and a round of golf often results in cracking big deals even with difficult colleagues. Still, he managed to beat his close friend and golfing rival, Billy, on several occasions on the ground of golf clinching the trophy from him in several amateur championships. Still, he always said that he never tried winning the games, he always tried not to lose what he had at stake in the game. So every game was a business for him. However, for Joy, golf was neither a business nor a game; it was an excuse for him to stay away from his father and stay close to Jas.

Jas and Joy both were aware of the golfing rivalry between their parents. But the chance has always made them stick together and appreciate each other. They also knew that it is their love for the game that has the power and possibilities of bringing their families together, someday. They passionately pursued their love for the game in the foreign land.

However, be it a game of golf or love, such games are played on the pitch of prospects. They are played against the odds of losing and the probabilities of winning. The possibility of winning keeps the player charged to give their best for the love of the game and the risks of losing make the game interesting and intriguing. If there is a set outcome for every move, if there is a fixed result for a measured effort, no game will be fun, and no one will want to play. Though every player is a possible winner, luck exists not to undermine the effort of the players but to make life and its games interesting.

In the game of love, however, nobody was ever a celebrated champion. Nobody ever found the winning mix, the formula, the code to follow for succeeding in the game of love. The game of love has remained mysteriously elusive and is unmastered, always leaving scopes for deeper dedication even on the part of the greatest lover. Hence Jas's hesitation was natural.

The game of love is one of the greatest of all games in life, but it is a game that is understood differently by different people. For some, it is the only game where winning is not important, while for some others winning is the only way out in love. Some consider everything is fair in love, while some prefer to play fair in love.

For Jas, it was a game of hope, where she hoped that Joy would get back to her sooner or later because she believed that her feeling of being together forever was not founded only on the common sport they cherished but because they had cherished the feeling of being together forever, which was love. It was love that had kept them together for all these years and brought them together to the same college in a foreign land. She thought that the recent drift of Joy from her was a mere test of her love for him and so she was hopeful that he will return to her as a passionate lover, eventually. In the game of love, hope is the key. It is the hope of winning the heart that keeps a player in the game. The moment one loses hope the game is over.

Nevertheless, like most games, the game of love too is played on a canvas of chance. There is no perfect course to follow in love, no sure strategy, no certain mix for a sure success. Though luck cannot be rid of the game, being a player herself Jas knew that if a player strategizes and works on one's skills, the better one is at removing luck from the game! The better one plays, the better are the chances of winning in a game.

She had let the chance take its course initially that led her to the brink and suddenly, she was scared to find herself at the loser's end in the game of love. Therefore, she gathered her guts and decided to take charge of her life and love and not let chance dictate its dictum. Consequently, she sought her aunt's support before it was too late. There was nobody better than Aunt Bubbles who could understand her and salvage her sinking heart. Jas, called up her aunt on the pretext of playing a round of golf with her, and there she swas for her niece, driving fifty miles.

Though Joy had been her golfing buddy since the time Jas began playing golf, but she learnt golf and its nuances from her aunt. If Joy gave her the courage and confidence to excel in the game by staying by her side, Aunt Bubbles was her inspiration to pursue the sport to its highest level. Every time she had an opportunity to play with Aunt Bubbles, Jas was the happiest girl.

As a kid, Jas grew up watching her aunt ravaging the turf and TV screens as a celebrity golfing star on Ladies Tour. She therefore often resorted to seeking help from her for fixing her swing, or for her game without the slightest doubt, but this time the game was different, it was love, and she knew not how to seek her help and swing through the situation successfully.

Bubbles teed off with her niece in the afternoon and by the time they were back, close to the clubhouse near the 18th green, she was privy to most of the college stories of Jas and Joy, initially, she was a little hesitant to share but after all, she was her closest confidante. She shared almost all the details of their time in the university, bit by bit in between the golf shots while walking together on the links except her deeper feelings for Joy.

Though she refrained from proclaiming her love for Joy, the emotions of her heart were betrayed by her eyes. Bubbles thought that her niece will be better off if she shares her heart with her, for that would redeem her from the emotional throes and pangs of the heart of young age.

When Jas was about to make her finishing putt on the final green, in a sort of abruptness, Bubbles questioned, 'Jas, it appears you are in love! ain't you?'

Jas who was hovering her putter on the ball for her putt, kept silent for a few moments and then struck the ball straight in the hole without a word, but when posed with such direct questions, people often vent out their emotion abruptly and so did Jas, she admitted, 'Yes, I am in love. I wish Joy not only to be my golf mate but soulmate too.'

Bubbles then stretched her arms and gave a tight hug to her niece on the 18th green, cheering her up, the deluge of emotions from her heart found a way eventually, her eyes were now all wet.

'Feelings for others should not be harboured in heart for too long, they should be conveyed to the one for whom they are meant,' the aunt comforted her niece with a piece of advice. 'For feelings are like seeds which can have an initial sprout in one's heart but to attain fruition they should reach the heart of a person for whom they are intended.'

She asked Jas, where would she find Joy.

Jas said, 'It is the last day of his Junket Tour with Liza, and he should be at the Casino Edin, of Edinburgh.'

The Game of Chance

In a game of chance, if one is on a losing spree, to get to the lowest pit of gambling he doesn't have to be at the famed Vegas Strip. Winning large may be limited to the wealthy clubs of Sin City but whenever people get playful, the vulnerability of losing sumptuously exists everywhere.

It was an old casino in a silent street of the Scottish capital, housed discreetly in a huge building in a corner of a street. The interiors of the building were shady and silent but from the outside, it was a specimen of art deco; with its whitewashed facade resembling a radiator grille of a classic American car. A bit odd-looking from the outside but the architecture; reminisces the rising consumerism, extravagance, and exuberance of the '30s.

The large gallery of the gaming zone was lined with slot machines. The gallery was illuminated with a glow of rosy redness emitted by the slots which were also the brightest object around. The warm yellow diffuse from the overhead illumination was soft and subtle, it let people see-through, but not see it whole.

Caverns of casinos are a world in themselves, they have a peculiar vibe that makes these places half-real and half-imaginary. In these gaming dens, it is an ambience of enchantment that keeps its visitors engaged, and lingering. Time passes and the ambience begins to work on the mood of the guests, restraint is not easy in such situations, and the player within often falls for the thrill of speculated rewards. Casinos are not a place to look for reality or morals, as one enters a gambling gallery, the world outside begins to turn hazy.

When Bubbles entered the Casino Edin, it was evening outside but within the building the time was static. Her eyes immediately began the search, she was looking for Joy, and after a little roving around, her eyes eventually settled in a gambling pit of the casino; there a stack of chips was staged to the vertical tipping height. The building was balancing delicately on the fringe of an oval poker table.

Within those time-less walls, surrounded by beautiful cocktail waitresses and freely flowing exquisite liquor, Joy, the only son of one of the wealthiest businessmen nearly lost his touch with reality. He pushed the tower towards the commit line into the live betting area of the poker table.

Be it on the table or on the turf, Bobby had a reputation of being the biggest punter in every game he played. Joy's father was known for keeping his stakes high, but it was never expected from him. He never indulged so deeply in a game of chance, particularly if relations were at stake. Also, his inclination to go against his father's way of living was evident from the very beginning of his childhood. He never endorsed his father's ambitious run for the money, a pursuit made at the cost of happiness of his close relations, and at times the relation itself.

His mother's demise in his early childhood particularly enraged his feelings against his father. It was not that he held his father responsible for his mother's death but it was his absence in her last hours that he felt unjustified. He somehow loathes his father's decision to go on a business trip when he should have chosen to stay with her ailing wife. She died in the absence of her husband but in front of her young son. The incident turned him into a silent rebel.

Time elapsed, and the father-son relations remained in a tight-rope balance. The father ensured that his son gets whatever money could buy and in return expected a respectful submission from his son. At the slightest call, there was a whole contingent of servants for Joy, all his needs were taken care of by paid attendants since childhood.

However, as he grew, he needed very few things, and fewer paid people around him. Especially, when he found his game and dedicated his life to golf, and when he found a companion in Jas, he wished for nothing more from the world. With time, the search for the father in the child's eyes was displaced by dreams of young emotions of adulthood. As time went by, often a telephonic call was the only connection they shared over long periods of time, and distances.

He had long been disregarding his father's insistence to see Mr Linn's daughter, Liza. However, a recent call from his father ruffled his rebellious streak again. Joy was told, rather informed about his prospective alliance with Liza. Bobby said that he had committed to Mr Linn for getting into a family alliance. He advised his son to date Ms Linn; it was not only necessary to honour his father's words but also for his own future. He explained how critical the alliance is for the future of the business empire which he is striving to expand for none other than his own son. He asserted that businesses become big when businessmen use brains instead of a heart. He asserted that it is time he grows up and start making decisions with his brain instead of blindly following his heart.

This time, the assertiveness of his father was too much for Joy, a disregard for his sentiments in matters of his personal life seemed to have incited a deep regress in him. And in such situations where infliction comes from the closest one, a man often does not retaliate by hurting back the person, instead, he resorts to hurting himself.

At the gambling table, Joy appeared to have been in a self-damaging mode as if drawing some sedative pleasure by sinking himself and thereby his father's ambitions, it certainly was not him but his stifled vengeance. It was obvious that the young man was hurt deeply.

Ambitions of a man determine his worth, but over ambitions often lead to despair. Bob's ambition to keep his business empire thriving offshores led him to get into a deal with one of the big real estate companies of the UK, and a secret deal with its promoter Mr Linn. As per the deal, Mr Linn was to facilitate the acquisition of his own company by Bob's company, while as per his covert commitment, in lieu of this favour Mr Bob has to marry his son, Joy to his daughter Liza, a strategic business alliance.

But when business and relations are attempted together, the proceedings are delicate. The repercussions of such attempts are not always pleasing. If they go wrong the outcomes of such alliances often are unexpected. However, blinded by prospects of huge business gains, Bobby was ushering his son into a prospective relationship with Liza; a relation in forming, but lacking the foundation of fidelity.

The disregard for his emotions from his father and his persuasion to get into a relationship with someone without any emotional connect, led Joy into the fold of nasty casino junkets. Motivated by the infinite depth of his father's pocket, a network of junkets and money lenders laid a lure for Joy. After all, he was the only son of one of the wealthiest businessmen in the world, and so was a potential star high roller for casino corridors.

The secret auto-active response system of Triads and Tongs, with their discrete links everywhere, alerted them of a presence of a wealthy whale in their vicinity. Though the Triads remain low profile and have no faces but still their extensive networks with junkets, high rollers, investors and criminals have gone obvious many a times, and Liza was one of the faces.

Liza owed a huge sum of debt to these lenders. Though these lenders often remain in the dark they do creep out when a vulnerable target is there in the vicinity. Once Liza was vulnerable, and now Joy was there in the snare, and once someone falls in their fold it is hard to get out of their web. She was now coerced to bring Joy to their playing dens.

Many roads lead to the world where dealings are dark and business shady but not all tread to these forbidden paths purposely. Sometimes situations lead to those lanes and at other times a sheer sweep of emotions throws a person into the dark dens. Liza too became an accomplice in the larger scheme as she was in emotional entanglements with Mr Reich. The man ran not only a casino junket tour operation company but also had dealings with the underworld, an aspect known less of him. He otherwise was a reputed businessman, he held shares in the company of Liza's father, and was there on the board as an influential member.

On getting the wind of the deal between Mr Linn and Bobby, Mr Reich got deeply disturbed not because he had stakes in his company but because his own scheme of acquiring Linn's company was in sudden jeopardy. He aspired to marry Liza who was the only heir of Mr Linn, which would have eventually made him the owner of the company, had his larger scheme would have reached fruition.

However, with ongoing developments, when he realized that acquiring the company through Liza was thinning out he decided to act quickly. He thought of giving an altogether different spin to future events. He cooked up a fresh plan and coerced Liza to help him execute it for the sake of their common future and relationship.

He organized a junket tour and asked Liza to convince Joy to accompany her on the pretext of getting to know each other better. He convinced her to lure him to gamble for fun initially so that eventually he trades the shares that he owns in his father's company to pay for a credit that he intended to grant him when he gets deep in debt while playing.

Liza realized the merit of the scheme, if it works, Bob's company would not be able to acquire her father's company for Joy would lose his shares to Mr Reich. She thought that this way she will be able to save her father's company and also her relationship with Mr Reich, the proposed marriage with Joy being purely a prospective business alliance would eventually fail if the business deal falters.

Liza's father, however, was keen on getting her engaged with Joy. He thought marrying her into a big business family would improve her prospects, and for that, he even agreed to compromise on his own business ethics. But Liza was deep down in an emotional relationship with Mr Reich and therefore obeyed him like a child, and as per plan, she lured the potential high roller to the doors of the casino.

Mr Reich primarily was a junket operator. Junkets are the mainstay for the survival of casinos; they ensure the right traffic keeps coming to the dens. They add to the fun element of the overall experience for the VIP guests, taking care of not only their accommodation but also any other needs that may arise. They ensure the flow of money by extending credit to the gamblers and assuming the responsibility of recovering what is owed, delicately or otherwise. In such opaque working environments, it is often hard to see the source of flowing funds.

Mr Reich functioned as a link between the world outside and the economy that ran in the dark through his junket tour company. It was certain that even if Joy don't return to the den a second time, even in a single shot he could be stripped significantly of his wealth, legally or otherwise. Liza thought that this would at least help her settle her own debts that she had to pay back to the lenders who operated through her boyfriend. On Liza's insistence, Joy agreed to go on a week-long trip with her.

Joy had just finished college and before he could have moved back to his homeland with Jas, his father's call changed the course of his life. Although Joy's feelings of friendship for Jas took an amorous turn over a period of time, being a reserved personality, he never dared to admit his love to her. He always doubted that if the same feelings were not there in Jas's heart, his admission would spoil even the friendly relations that they nurtured since childhood.

His thoughts kept him entangled in an emotional quandary for a long time and he never succeeded in summoning the courage to speak his heart, perhaps he was waiting for Jas to listen to the call of his heart. However, Jas too hid her feelings and never expressed her heart to Joy, even at the news of him being engaged to Liza. This made Joy believe in the destiny decided by his father for him, eventually, he gave in to the insistence of his father and let destiny take its course. He left for the decided junket tour, and with a heavy heart asked Jas to fly back home.

He thought that leaving life in the hands of destiny would eventually unwind and redeem him emotionally. Instead, he got entwined further in the game of chance. He had already lost 50 million Dollars to the house on the culminating day of his junket tour at the Casino Edin. It was, however, not the loss of money only but the trap was about extracting the shares of his own company.

For receiving a credit line from the House, he eventually traded his shares to continue with the game in Casino Edin and was deep in the trap laid by the junkets. It was not a sane decision for sure, and Bubbles could see that the young boy was not in his senses. He appeared to have been heavily under the influence of alcohol, possibly drugged and dragged in the murky muck of forced gambling.

Bubbles accosted him, 'Joy, is this your game?'

Joy turned towards the voice, and after realizing that Aunt Bubbles was there, turned back silently.

Bubbles questioned again, 'Is this your pursuit, how can you be so careless?'

'I am not on any pursuit, and I have no one to care for', Joy muttered in a low tone.

'Obviously, like father, like son.'

Joy looked at Aunt Bubbles, again, and said, 'I am not like my father.'

'If it is so, you would have cared for Jas, who has been waiting for you all through this week, in pain, and you are having a fun trip.'

'I told her to fly back home, from here our ways part. Now, my life is on a different course.'

'That's what makes you like your father. You are blind to see how much someone loves you, but for you, business deals matter, not love!'

Listening to this, Joy looked back again.

'Alright, I will let her know that all these years she had loved a man who is determined to go his own way; the way of business and money.'

After a pause, Joy hesitantly repeated, 'Does she love me? Did she say this to you!'

'Of course, she confessed to me that you are not only her golf mate but also her love. But now I doubt, whether she would love a gambler as much as she loved a golfer!'

Joy stood from his chair, pulled up his phone, and dialled. He slowly walked away, talking, looking for privacy in the noisy galleries of the Casino Edin.

Bubbles also dialled a number, the phone was picked and she spoke, 'Hello, Bob.'

'Hello, who is this?', the voice responded back.

'Bob, I am Bubbles!'

There was a brief pause, for a few moments.

Bobby, then asked, 'Yes, Bubbles, is everything all right? What made you remember me!'

'Everything is fine with me Bob, but it appears, with you still many things are not fine! You may keep money above all your relations but how can you trade the happiness of your own son?'

In a concerned tone, Bobby asked, 'What is the matter with Joy, is he alright? Where is he?'

'You are his father; you should know where is he and how he is! Bobby, even if you are pardoned for your past, all your life you would regret heartily if you fail as a father.'

'Bubbles, tell me what is the matter, I don't understand what you are talking about!'

'Bobby, your son is here in the Edin and for the last one week he has been on a losing spree, it is not only the gambling that is ripping you and him of wealth but it appears your indifferent attitude is ripping your son with all the happiness he was seeking silently for all these years. You were never there for him, but now you should not deprive him of the very happiness he has been aspiring for all through his life. Poker is not his game, golf is. And

Liza is not her love, Jas is. You should understand this, otherwise you will lose your son forever.'

The conversation continued for long and Bubbles eventually made him realize that he was at fault for not seeing what was obvious in his son. Bobby got scared at the thought of losing Joy, his only true relation left, the rest all were there for his wealth only.

Bobby got desperate to provide his son with what he wished and let him choose his own life, and his own love. However, he felt helpless at the thought that even if he bends, Billy will not agree to marry his daughter Jas, to his family.

His unlimited wealth suddenly appeared worthless to him as he realized that it could not buy happiness for his son. At this thought, for the first time, he felt wretched. He somehow wanted to do whatever it takes to save his son from slipping from his life, for the happiness of Joy, he was now ready to surrender his ego and even the 18th green.

He broke before Bubbles, and beseeched her to somehow convince Joy to get back to him, and to his game of golf. He told her that he is sponsoring the National Open Golf Tournament in the capital that is scheduled in the next few weeks, and all this he is doing, is for his son. He wished to introduce him to the golfing world through this tournament at his home club.

Further, Bobby acknowledged that probably he never understood his son and his feelings all these years, but now he does not want to part with his real wealth, his son Joy, nor could he commit the sin of being a reason of ruining his happiness. He, therefore, pleaded her to convince Billy, her brother, to consider marrying Jas to his son for the happiness of the children.

However, Bubbles knew that his brother would not agree to it if approached straightforwardly. She, however, decided to take charge of orchestrating the future events of the game of life of two young golfers. She knew that after all, life too is a game of strategy, and a lot could be achieved with timely intervention and action.

She told Bob that she is sending both of them back the next day, and asked him to take care of his son as a father rather than a businessman. She also assured him that at an appropriate time she would convince his brother for the alliance of the two. Bubbles told him that she would talk to Billy about the matter when she would see him in person. She further added that she would be visiting the capital for the upcoming National Open Golf Tournament.

Playing Together

It was an early morning in the capital and most of the city dwellers were still asleep. The golfers, however, were the exception who rose before the sun. The golfers had begun to pour at the two courses of the capital; the CGC and DLGR, even in the early morning darkness. Soon the horizon ushered a yawning sun in hues of reds, possibly pursuing the enthusiasm of golfers.

As the build-up of golfers continued on the two courses, the sun slowly toned the sky from smoky-black to blue. The colours of landscape and shades of green turf acquired their true tints slowly, and golfers their cheerful humour. A picture-perfect morning with a slow-blowing breeze augured well for the first day of the National Open week. In the capital, the Pro-Am day dawned crisp and clear!

Pro-Ams are one of the most exciting events attached to golf tournaments and are particularly of interest to amateur golfers. Pro-Ams generally mark the inaugural day of a week-long golfing tournament, however, the excitement of this single day is no less than the actual tournament. Naturally, this day was long-awaited by the members of the two clubs who received the invite for Pro-Am. They felt no less than a VIP because they knew that it ensured access to most areas which otherwise are exclusive to the Tour Pros. They knew that the Pro-Am invite is a ticket to get closest to being on tour at least for a day.

In golf, a Pro-Aam is a tournament that is played amongst professionals and amateurs. Every group typically has a professional and four amateur partners who compete as a best ball fivesome. The lavish parties and grand award functions associated with Pro-Ams are a certain attraction for club golfers. However, the craze for playing with the world's best professional golfers is no less.

Therefore, members of the two clubs, who were the Ams for the tournament, arrived at their designated golf course on time. They were enthusiastic to meet their allotted Pro golfer. The action began to unfold as each team headed towards the teeing grounds, they were ready to tee up and put their game to the test. The morning stir got intense by the afternoon as amateurs and professionals tested their metal in the two signature golf courses of the capital. The Pros continued to pour in the two courses as per their scheduled tee-off times, and the morning bloomed further. However, it was not the morning but the last evening where the tone for the event was set with one of the most opulent pairing parties.

A gala party was organized on the lavish lawns of DLGR, the previous evening. The members of the two clubs, CGC and DLGR, who received the exclusive invitation for the pairing party reached the clubhouse on time. The excitement was high not only because the party was a show of grandeur in itself, but because the world's best golfers descended in the capital for the first time in such large numbers. Having an opportunity to choose a golfing star of choice for playing with him even for a day was a dream coming true for many.

A drawing party where amateurs are paired with professionals is always an exciting experience for participants. For the party, exclusive invites were sent not only to the club members of the two courses but also to golfers from all walks of life.

The invitees included hall-of-fame actors and athletes, Chairpersons of businesses and bureaucracy, politicians, and professionals, and the members of the two clubs who lent their golf courses for the event sacrificing their own play for a week. However, Bob had aptly compensated the club members by throwing one of the finest pairing parties ever witnessed by the golfers of the capital. It was a party to remember.

At the party, as the draw progressed so did the excitement amongst the participating guests. Slowly the world's best players who were available for the Pro-Am were picked up, followed by the lesser-known ones. Although the top few were pre-selected by the sponsors and were not available for the lottery, still every pro playing in the tournament was a potential champion.

At Pro-Am pairing parties, Though, Ams require some luck to get the Pros of choice through the lottery system but fun activities, entertainment, exclusive gifts, and an opulent set of freebies remain on offer to one and all. Nevertheless, for admirers of the game, collecting player and caddie badges, and a fancy pass for a week are the most prized pieces.

Being a President of the host Club and a key sponsor of the event, Bobby had the privilege to pre-select one of the top-ranking professionals of the world, but for his Pro-Am group, he chose his own son, Joy who was there in the tournament. However, he secured his slot in the event by being the champion of the recent 'National Amateur Championship', and not through the sponsor's quota.

On Pro-Am day, a galaxy of stars descended on the turf of the two courses. The celebrities were from all walks of life; literature, entertainment, politics, bureaucracy, business, and even from other sports like cricket and football. After all, golf is a game that has its admirers everywhere, people from all walks of life. It is a sport played by all, young and old irrespective of age, the only eligibility to get onto the field is to have a spirit for sport.

Golfing greats are always a celebrity for an amateur golfer, but in this celebrity-rich event, even a fellow amateur was a star of some kind. So, the members of the two clubs awaited the event with eagerness for they had a chance to see the swing of their favourite star from up close. Watching them play in their carefree style, walking by their side was a goosebump experience for the fans.

The golf courses transformed into a kind of a stellar stage on the day of the Pro-Am. The most decorated footballer, the god of cricket, and the godfather of the silver screen, all big shots of the world and entertainment industry were on the same turf. It was a rare occasion when the celebrities of sport, showbiz, and golf were all together; having fun and frolicking with their friends and families.

The courses during the event were more like fun villages, and the day looked like a funfair; hoops of basketball, a pavilion for striking football, and a stage to act and entertain. All kinds of activities were tried in the golf village to entertain visitors with varying tastes. The citizens of the capital were surprised to see that golf could be such fun, even for casual visitors of the course.

On the day of the Pro-Am, golf courses have peculiar vibes, players just play for the sake of experience and winning is not their primary objective. Spectators throng the galleries to take a closer look at their star golfers. Pro-Ams are the days when Pros are relatively casual in their game and often don't mind signing autographs to their fans or shaking hands if they are close to the gallery. Fans too have relatively more freedom on the day to roam around the course casually and have fun, therefore it is enjoyed equally by amateurs, professionals, and spectators too.

Playing a golf course that is set up to the tour standards where the big shots of the game are about to compete. Playing with the golfing stars observing their game closely and witnessing them lead you to the hole is an exclusive experience, such an opportunity is rare unless one is playing a Pro-Am where professionals and amateurs share the same turf and appreciate each other's love for the game, equally.

Imagine a feeling, when you are on a green confused, the green is breaking and a top professional standing next to you helps you read the contours or tells you how to extract a ball from sand when you land in a bunker. These lessons learned may not improve your game altogether but by playing a Pro-Am your appreciation and affection for the game may certainly be enhanced.

On the two courses, the day-long festivity came to a conclusion, and participants geared up for another star-studded evening. The week-long event was organized in a two-course format. Some of the events were to be held at DLGR while others were scheduled at CGC. The prize distribution ceremony of the Pro-Am was to be held at the classic clubhouse of CGC. The dais was richly decorated, having presidents of the two host clubs, Bob and Billy, along with other sponsors, promotors, and key personnel involved in organizing the mega event.

The high-power stage was handled by Bubbles, the witty woman of CGC as she was known in the golfing club circles in her heydays. She, however, was not short of wits even in the present times, and at the dais, she represented her News Network as a celebrity anchor. She was there in the role of compere, rather than Billy's sister. However, only she herself knew that her presence at the dais was necessary not for the golf event but for setting the course of events in the right direction for the good of the two clubs, two old friends and two young golfers.

She thought that if she could succeed in having public commitments from Bob and from Billy, in particular, they would honour their words. And if those commitments somehow could culminate in the nuptial knots of Jas and Joy, the rivalry between the two families will be resolved forever. It will not bring the two old friends together again but also two clubs, and would also pave way for the good of the game in the capital.

The audience was highly charged, and Bubbles managed the dais with the best of her wits. She could do only so much as the situation may permit in such matters of interwoven emotions. She knew that in the game of life, intelligent interference could lead to desired results but until the results are out, all such attempts in the real world are mere means of improving the odds. The actual outcomes are decided by time. Therefore, to know the future for sure one has to wait for the time, with patience and hope, and she was very hopeful.

The ongoing golf competition in the capital was not only amongst the golfers but in essence, was between the two rival golf clubs. Though in golf, rooting is not as loud as in other sports of aggression, still, when it is a competition, even golf fans have a tendency to root for their home players with greater enthusiasm. Therefore, the rooters of the two clubs tried to dominate each other with a competitive air of superiority.

Jas's brother Jem, represented the rich golfing legacy of CGC. He was not only the defending champion of the title but also a reigning world champion. On the other hand, DLGR was represented by Jas's close friend, Joy, who was playing his debut pro event. However, he was not only the winner of the Pro-Am tournament but also a rookie star who recently won 'The National Amateur Championship'. In his debut professional event, he appeared all set to challenge the supremacy of CGC with the fine display of his unmatched golfing skills.

Bubbles was looking for an opportunity to pit Bob and Billy against each other and she got one after the prize distribution. There was a media interaction and sensing the opportunity Bubbles put her wits to work, and on a lighter note, she said, 'Bobby, you are often heard saying that unless there is something at stake that is worth fighting, nobody plays his best games!'

'Yes, you heard it right,' said Bobby.

'Also, it is popular that you have never played a game in your life without a bet.'

'Well, it is one of the many things that makes me popular, I bet', responded Bob.

The conversation was getting interesting for the people present and they were now paying more attention to the talks taking place at the dais.

Bubbles coaxed the brash Bobby a little more with her words and said, 'This time, the two clubs are against each other, and one of them is yours. Don't you have anything at stake in this tournament to make it worth fighting for the golfers of the two clubs?'

'Well, when you know so much about me you must be aware that I always offered the honour of choosing my stakes to my adversary, and then I decided the stakes for my opponent. This somehow ensured that I had worthy adversaries in all games of my life.'

'So you mean, the CGC club should come forward to decide your stakes', added Bubbles, quickly.

'For worthy opponents, I don't mind offering the same honour, even today', Bob responded firmly in front of the packed party room and media cameras.

She then turned to his brother, president of CGC, 'Billy, would you like to dictate stakes for Bob, for this tournament.'

In the spur of the moment, Billy said, 'Jem is representing our club, so I authorize him to attend to the challenge.'

Jem picked up the mic and said, 'For Mr Bobby, the 18th green of CGC will be at stake.'

There was a huge thunder of applause and to this, Bob had no other option but to agree with a smile.

Now it was Billy's turn to declare his stake.

Bubbles asked, 'Billy, what would you like to put at stake on your behalf.'

Charged with a competitive mindset, without much thinking Billy said, 'golf is a game of equals and as Jem decided Mr Bob's stakes, I give my words to Joy, he may ask whatever he likes from me, who represents DLGR. As per the tradition of golf, CGC knows how to keep parity in the game.'

Bubbles was happy at the thought that so far the course of conversations was going the way she desired. It was now Joy's turn, and she had already drilled in his head that whenever the time comes and he is offered an opportunity by Billy to ask for something from him, he should not miss the opportunity of asking for Jas's hand, without wavering. This was the moment for Joy to proclaim his love in front of the entire world.

Bubbles looked straight into the eyes of Joy and prompted him to ask for his heart's wish, her look intensified to save Joy from a falter at the final moment. Keeping focused eye contact, in a deep voice, Bubbles asked him, 'Joy, what you want from Mr Billy, speak your heart.'

After a little pause, Joy said, 'I want the hand of your daughter. We are in love and I wish to marry her.'

For a moment, there was silence, then commotion, but Mr Billy kept his calm and said, 'Daughters from our family marry only champions, and a worthy champion will have the hand of my daughter.'

'May the love prevail, and may it win', said Bubbles with an intent to support Joy's proposal in public and build pressure on her brother to agree to it.

However, Billy's reply was terse, 'Winning a championship is different than winning a Pro-Am trophy! Anyway, I honour the bet with which we are bound now.'

Thursday

It was the early morning of a tranquil Thursday, and the dawn was yet to break. The golf course was silently dark and the club quarters quiet. The only building lit and visible at that hour of the morning was the maintenance shop of DLGR. Then, there was a movement. At the exit of the maintenance shed there appeared lights, moving lights, which slowly began to march on the road leading to the golf course.

It seemed as if some contingent took a charge of illuminating the course by borrowing light from the fluorescence that brightened the workshop building. The bunch of scintillates that were issued from the exit door moved in a disciplined linear formation for some distance on the main road, and then furcated randomly, spreading out in different directions of the course.

The illuminating dots in distance were the headlights of machines and headlamps worn by the greenkeepers. They were on their way to the golf course for their routine job of mowing and maintaining the turf; a prime asset for any golf course.

Once off from the shop, they began to spread quickly all over the course. Like fireflies at play, they hopped from one green to the other, zipping hurriedly from one fairway to another, crisscrossing through secret paths that existed in the intervening forests, known best to them. At one point in time, they frantically raced in a fairway but after a few minutes of the show, suddenly disappeared in the forest, and then again emerged at the other end of the thicket, tracing the tracks of another fairway to finish its mowing.

Call it their skills, experience, intuition, or their sheer passion for their job, mounted high on mammoth machines, they found their ways skilfully through darkness and forest. They mowed the turf with geometric precision even when it was pitch dark.

In the early morning darkness, the turf below and the sky above appeared as one continuous course, stretched endlessly in all directions. However, the hovering lanterns on the turf and twinkling stars in the sky appeared as one team at work, trying together to dispel the darkness. They seemed determined like the greenkeeping crew to set the pitch with perfection for the game that is played on it, every day, for ages.

Under the supervision of the course superintendent, the team of greenkeepers worked in sync with quickness. One team was on its mission to mow all the 18 greens, others looked after the tees, and one another team mowed fairways in a spread of two-hundred odd acres of the land, that too in torchlights. The feat accomplished was not only about mowing greens but for achieving tabletop surfaces they were also to be rolled. A crew with rolling machines followed the mowers to accomplish the task perfectly and quickly, for they also had to move out of the way before any golfer tees his ball on the course.

The first two days of the four-day National Open tournament were scheduled to be played at the DLGR and the last two days at the CGC. Even on normal days, the maintenance standards of the two courses were always under scrutiny and comparison of the golfers who played the two courses. Green conditions in the rival courses always were a matter of debate amongst members not only in boardrooms but on the ground too. Therefore now, when one of the biggest tournaments was due to be played on the two courses, a comparison from the golfers was expected for sure.

It was certain that during the National Open, the course presentation would be judged in broad daylight by the entire world; by the visiting golfers of the world, and the golfing fans who will watch it on TV, for the tournament were to go live globally. Hence, in the two courses, every member of the greenkeeping crew was prepared to put in his best effort, and outperform the rivals from the other club. The competition was not only amongst the golfers but also between the greenkeepers of the two courses.

The crew of the DLGR wanted to showcase its best craft ever, they were careful not to leave any stone unturned and keep the flag of their course high, particularly higher than the course across the road where the last two rounds of the tournament were scheduled to be played.

Though, the application of cut at the end of the first two days was sure to screen almost half of the players, yet, the other half of the field was certain to play the other course. The players at the end of their game are inclined to speak about their experience, if not winners, then the less fortunate ones who fail to make a mark in the event do often feel like sharing their opinions.

Eventually, the horizon got lit by the rising sun, and the finely cut turf glistened with its ruler-drawn stripes, a testament to the craft performed by a skilful band. The orchestrated performances of greenkeepers are however often missed by golfers because by the time they enter the course the crew often is on its beating retreat.

The mowers, the rollers, and the maintenance crew were seen trailing towards the shed, in a queue, disappearing slowly into obscurity. But before receding back to the shop, they accomplished their job to perfection; the striped fairways looked fantastic, the greens were slick and shiny, and in bunkers, the sand was raked uniformly that glistened like gold dust in the morning sun. The two signature golf courses of the capital which were just an earshot apart were ready to host the greatest show of golf.

In the parking lot of the club, multiple cars were busy conveying groups of golfers from their hotels to the club. With the arrival of the courtesy cars, traffic picked up. The cars were the same brand and all white, and so was the livery of the chauffeurs that was becoming on them. The colourfully dressed players who alighted from these cars, however, added vibrant hues to the grassy green canvas of the course.

Golfers gathered on the freshly mown turf of practice areas. The greens appeared fast. Golf balls rolled with blitzing speeds on the practice greens in all directions, some sinking straight while others missing the targeted holes. The driving range steadily got abuzz with the tinkers of golf balls which were shot in succession from its bays. The stage was all set for the biggest golf tournament in the golfing history of the capital.

The draw sheet for the first round of the tournament was pinned next to the Local Rules, neatly on the notice board of the tournament office. It was a two-tee start, on the first two days the field was large and so it was an obvious decision to finish the play on time. As per the scheduled tee-off, the golfers' groups headed to their respective tees.

The first teeing ground of the DLGR was a sprawling green carpet, after all, it was intended to be a gateway to a magnificent course. With its vast spread of velvety turf cut to diamond pattern, it became the entry it signified for a grand course. The tee was set up befittingly for the occasion, the checkerboard turf of the tee was framed neatly with colourful boards of brandings. The branding boards of the National Open and event sponsors ran all along its margins. The signature green Rolex dial was also tucked at one side of the tee.

A starter, wearing a green jacket, looked sharp in his presentation, he came forward with a cordless mic in one hand and a drawsheet in the other. He announced the name of the first professional golfer with clear pronunciation. As a golfer ascended to the tee, a huge round of applause reverberated energising the ambience. The golfer reciprocated the enthusiasm of supporters with a smile on his face and a little bow of the head, however, as he walked forward to tee up, a pin drop silence seeped through the surroundings.

The discipline in the game of golf is its real charm, even the fans of the game know when to cheer and when to go calm. The spectators froze in their places to avoid disturbing the player while he performed his shot. The concern for the player's game by the galleries and that of a player to his fellow competitor makes this game unique. In the field, every player knows that his greatest adversary is he himself, not the opponent with whom he is grouped to play the course.

On the first tee, a ball was teed up, then with an absolute focus and perfect swing, it was struck giving it a long and lofty flight. Eventually, the golf ball landed in the centre of the fairway, and again loud applause from the spectators who gathered around the first tee, pervaded all over. The National Open golf tournament has officially begun in the capital.

The other players of the group also repeated similar performances one after the other as their golf balls too kissed the fair spots of the fairway. When each golfer of the group was done with his tee shot they began their walk briskly, straight to the fairway where their balls lay. A chunk of fans hived off from the swarm of spectators and began following their favourite players in the staked-out gallery.

Every few minutes the starter introduced a group of golfers who moved to the tee one by one to start their day and their pursuit for the title. However, each golfer was cheered by the spectators at the first tee grandstand. A round of applause from the fans was a real encouragement that helped them keep their spirits high throughout the day.

On the large TV screens, in contrast to the green turf, colourfully dressed players and their shots streamed continuously. In silence, the fans saw the leaders in making at different holes of the course. Digital leaderboards were installed at all prominent locations of the course on which stats of scores flashed every now and then keeping everybody updated about the progress of the tournament.

All the top golfers of the world irrespective of their nationalities are an attraction for golfing fans but there is an inner urge in every fan to see his local home club athlete shine to the occasion. Therefore, though, at the event, there were several star golfers worthy of large galleries but in the capital, the highest craze was there for the two local boys, Joy and Jem.

On the scale of experience and career track, both were at the opposite ends. Joy was just an amateur with a recent amateur championship in his name while Jem, on the other hand, was one of the top reigning professional golfers of the world, he had multiple titles already to his credit. Still, this year for the 'National Open' title, the fans were hoping to see young Joy, a worthy claimant.

Irrespective of the spectrum of star golfers, most spectators were interested in the two local boys, particularly in Joy. Not only because they represented the two golf clubs and their rivalry in the capital but also because they witnessed an incredible golfer in Joy. Fans saw a possible champion in Joy because he had displayed all characteristics of a one, in recent amateur tournaments. The speculations and hopes were high, for real.

When it was time for Joy and Jem to tee off, a large crowd was already thronging around, the grandstand was all packed. The duo approached the first tee and the sea of spectators cheered with full fervour. Joy hit his first shot with a firm grip, and perfect focus, landing in the fairway. Jem also followed him with a firm resolve that befitted a champion. As the two headed on their hunt for their golf balls, from the tee surrounds rivers of spectators split and began to flow as galleries along the staked ropes. The stir of spectators however went still at every shot, observing pin-drop silence to witness their players' performance on turf within the ropes.

The last group teed off from the first tee, and the field was complete. As the day progressed, the crowd also kept building up in the course. Some fans circled the tees while others were seen ringing around the greens, and some others preferred to move in blocks with their favourite player's group.

When the field was full and the game was on, every player was busy in his own game, seeking a fluttering flag, heading to the hole of his green. The whole pursuit appeared a repetitive loop; cyclic, vicious, and unending, with no beginning and no end, a familiar one. Certainly, the game is not new, it has already been played many a time, is it not?

As the day's game reached its crescendo, the entire course was abuzz with zestful cheers and soulful sighs, the emotions were so interwoven that it was hard to discern whom they belonged to; spectators or the players.

Golf is a game where fans too participate with players, they live every moment in the game together. The two experience the game simultaneously as it goes, on the same ground, sharing each moment live; spectators cheer at the sight of every good shot and moan at every miss of hole by a player's ball on the green.

Spectators of golf, largely wish to see players succeed at their game, irrespective of the camp he comes from. But certainly, if the leaders of a game are his favourites or from his home club, the pleasure of watching them lead is no less than bliss. Even in the distance, spurts of happiness and bursts of sighs were heard loudly as the game approached its culmination for the day.

At DLGR, golfing fans marvelled not only at the skills of the golfers but also at the scale of the sprawling course. Golf certainly is a memorable social event for any visitor, whether one treads the turf for being a participant or just walks in as a casual visitor. Golf courses are awe-inspiring places, a sheer size of a golf course often leaves first-time visitors spellbound.

They are also awe-struck to witness the scale of a golfing event; a game played simultaneously by hundreds of players on a boundless pitch that ranges from fine turf to rough terrains of all kinds, forests, and creeks. The wind, rain, and the Sun, all elements, everything being a part of the challenge, a pitch that tests the real metal of players. To add further to the oddity of the game, it is a game in which the responsibility of keeping the scores rests with a player, not the referees.

In the game, the players are not alone in their journey of eighteen holes. Their fans and supporters are always close to them, following their game throughout the course from the first tee to the finishing green. However, some like to walk by the side of the players, while others prefer to settle on a spot, lying idle on the mounds of turf, watching the action casually while sunbathing. Some choose to lounge on the lawns with kids and family while others enjoy the game from the cosy couch of their private pavilions, overlooking the finishing green.

In the game, though, a player is responsible for his shot and score but the course is always under the scrutiny of the spectators' eyes. Every shot is seen keenly by the fans of the game and every golfer is expected to keep up with the spirit of the game, in all fairness. It is therefore ensured that no one misses any detail of the tournament, the highlights of the ongoing game are streamed live on digital screens all over the course. Spectators act as an integral part of the game, adding actual adrenaline to the game, and appreciating its moments of highs and lows, equally.

The game and the course were a treat for spectators. The first day of the tournament was enjoyed heartily by everyone. Everyone had an intimate experience of nature where they got introduced to the course and the playing field. The beauty of the game and that of the course were appreciated wholeheartedly by every single visitor.

For players, however, the first day of the tournament was about keeping nerves and consistency in their game. On an inaugural day, most players try to toe the rhythm of the course and attempt to sync their own game with it. Golf is a game of resonance and synergy; if the course, the player, and the game all fall in harmony, success is a natural outcome, an effortless journey of happiness and bliss.

By the end of the day, the scorecards for the day were already signed and submitted by most players. However, irrespective of their day's performance most of them were hopeful for the next day, for the event had just begun, and everybody had at least one more day to amend any errors, if they inadvertently committed on the opening day. There was still one full round left for the cut, and to stay in contention!

As the last group of players submitted their scorecards, the first round of the National Open concluded. The final leaderboard was flush with the world's top reigning stars, including Jem whose name secured its place in the top ten rows. The upper section of the leaderboard had scores in bold letters in rich red, representing a horde of birdies that the top players must have shot while playing the holes. Joy was several rows down with a mix of blue and black figures, however, his overall score for the round was under par.

The game of golf is a game of strategy but ironically even the champions of the game remain in a continuing pursuit of figuring out the right strategy for their game. The scheme that works on one day may not work on the other day, and the tactics that rendered results in a particular golf course may not be helpful on another course. In fact, every day is a new day, a new game in the course, there is no absolute strategy ever known for ensuring success in the game, and that is what makes it interesting and also fair.

So some players in the game are aggressive from the very beginning while others prefer to play it for the par. Though every player aspires for birdies and eagles, it is natural to have pars too in the game. Even the champions of the game have their share of occasional bogeys and lows. It appeared that Joy resisted the initial inner drive of shooting birdies that most player has; instead, he chose to pursue pars for most of the holes. This approach to the game placed him amongst the average players on the leaderboard on the first day.

However, the game is not about a single day. The actual score is about the aggregate of all strokes that are attempted throughout the event, and it is the satisfaction on the last day that matters most in such games.

Friday

The early morning on Friday was foggy, and the same was forecasted for the weekend too! But, after sometime the day dawned bright. The blowing winds seemed to have swept the fog ushering the day with decent visibility. Had the fog not cleared with wind, it would have resulted in start delays; a nightmare for tournament organizers. It leads to logistical complications not only to organizers but everyone involved.

The wind, however, is a challenge to the players. A golfer not only faces competition from the field but also from weather. Out of all other elements, wind is the most notorious one that could render a quick burn to the scorecard of a golfer, who is otherwise performing well. It could quickly dash the dreams of even the most seasoned golfers in case he fails to negotiate with blowing winds, with precision and patience.

Winds turn out to be a most brutal element, especially in a golf course like DLGR, where the turf and water are merged aggressively to create a challenging golf track. It is a course where ample water exists, be it in the form of narrow inconspicuous creeks or wide-open large lakes, ready to devour any tiny ball that might have been amiss, even by a whisker.

In golf, whenever a golfer gets into the love triangle of wind, water, and greens, the outcomes are often unpredictable! The thrill and challenge for a golfer lies in clenching the greens from the wind and water. Anyway, in such a challenging scenario, whether he comes out playing par or otherwise, there is always a satisfaction of playing against worthy opponents.

Well, it is not only the weather that makes golf a brutal beauty but if one has the eyes to observe the fickleness of the game, he would see the silent but continued confrontations of a golfer with the game. There are other dimensions as well to the game which often are not obvious. Apparently, it is the same game and the same course even on the second day too, but it was a different day, a day where the game was largely a battle for survival. Nevertheless, battles for survival are mostly brutal, and golf is no exception. So if some say that the game is a cruel one, then they are not outrightly wrong!

Its cruelty becomes obvious, particularly on the second day of the tournament when a cut is applied. Though, each professional tour in the world has its own specifics for executing it on the ground, in simple terms, a cut in golf is about cutting the playing field to about half of the players. Now imagine more than a hundred players in a tournament of which about half are cut out from the event on the finish of the second day based on the aggregate scores of the total field.

Also, we know that professional golfers have to travel to new places, new cities, and new countries to participate in the events that happen on different golf courses in a year. Out of the thousands of professional golfers in the world, only a select few might have sponsors' support while all others have to bear all their travel costs, lodging and equipment costs, and also the tournament registration fee, each time, unlike the other sports. Is it not brutal?

If not so, then to further put it up in perspective, typically pro golfers earn a tournament paycheck only if they make a cut and the major chunk of the prize money is bagged by the top performers only leaving limited money to the players at the bottom of the ranking list. Further, even to maintain a tour card and remain eligible to participate in professional events, one has to remain in the top list of golfing tours, all at personal costs and efforts, does it sound brutal, now?

The tour has its rules and cut scores are necessary norms. Therefore on the second day, behind the entertaining show of rolling balls on the turf, it was a frenetic race of survival amongst players. Only the best of the lot would qualify to play two more days and finish the game on the fourth day.

The cutline is a dreaded zone, which can give nightmares even to the champions. On most tours and tournaments, if they miss the cut, they have no other way but to pack up and head back home after the second day of the tournament. The cut is a major scare for any golfer because failing to make a cut is not only about the average or ordinary golfers of the game, but it is a fairly routine thing in professional golf. Even the reigning champions of the world are not spared from its scorch because in spite of all skills and focus a player may fail in the game on the second day if he is short of the other spice for success called luck. Nevertheless, in the long run, we know that in the game the harder one works the luckier he gets. The better a pro golfer the fewer times he misses the cutline in a season or in his career.

Professional golf follows the principle of 'perform or perish', golfers who could not contain their nerves lose the opportunity to continue in the tournament after the conclusion of the second day. After the cut is applied, there may be times in a golf tournament when even the defending champion is no longer left in the field to defend the title anymore.

However, at DLGR, during the National Open, with a display of consistent performance Jem, the defending champion of the title, and the youngest challenger for it, Joy, both cleared the cut. The second-day leaderboard witnessed a lot of ups and downs with regard to the shift in positions and ranks of players with respect to the previous day. The reshuffle of names was quick on the board; some dropped, a few faded while a few others got bolder by the end of the day, probably the winds played their trick. It is a game where reconciliation with elements is rewarded quickly, and the key is adaptability to the conditions. But, eventually, the one who deserves, gets the slice of success.

However, if we pause and ponder a little, we realize that success means different things to different players in the field. For some, it may be a mere paycheck, while for others the game could be a struggle for survival. Amateurs hit the golf ball for the trophy and professionals for money. It could be a fun stroll for some and others may have their dearest things at stake and every shot on the golf ball could be a serious event in their life. Therefore, for every player, it is a personal pursuit and a unique one too.

Whoever is there in the game, has his own reasons and approach to deal with it, but Joy was there not for the purse which was largely sponsored by his own father neither was he playing his usual game for the sheer pleasure of playing it, but this time his stakes were different. Though he played most of his games without worrying about the results, this time he was finding it difficult to resist, a streak of restlessness kept running through his mind every now and then.

In this tournament, Joy's love was at stake—his very happiness, Jasmine. He had no option but to play his best game, however, the real challenge for him this time was not the game, but to play it without thinking about its outcome!

Hard work, practice, training, and all other strategies could help in improving the odds of winning the game of golf, but in the end, it is a game of uncertainty, particularly its outcome which is never in the control of the player. Even the toughest and the most seasoned champions of the game struggle continuously to remain at the top, or what many people call the zone. The game is fickle and has always changed its champion sooner or later. Though the game remains the same for ages, every round is a new round. Even for champions, it has always been an elusive pursuit, with every tee-off, it is a new chase.

At the end of Friday's round, Joy posted an aggregate score of -4, and Jem carded an aggregate score of -5. So, by the end of the second day Joy too had ascended on the leaderboard and secured his position in the top ten players of the tournament stating his contention firmly for the Saturday and Sunday rounds, and to the title. Though there were three more players on top of them with scores of -6, -7, and -7, still the fans could foresee an interesting game brewing up in the tournament. They were hoping to witness a tight struggle on the weekend.

As soon as the last group entered the scoring area to submit their cards, the show at DLGR was over. The event organizers and the TV crew were then seen winding up their setup hurriedly which anyway continued till late evening. Now, the spotlights were to shift to the old classic course of the capital, the CGC, where the other half of the adventure and the culmination of the mega event was scheduled.

Saturday

The Saturday Sun seemed reluctant to rise on the turf of CGC, it was already thirty minutes past the scheduled tournament tee-off time. The tournament was delayed already by half an hour due to poor visibility. But a thick shroud of fog stubbornly kept the course undercover. Though the greenkeeping crew of CGC had set up the course on time, and the course was in perfect condition, the weather, however, was not!

The Tournament Director reviewed the conditions again and announced a further delay of thirty more minutes. Even in the late morning, fairways beyond fifty yards were not visible. With sunset, set for 17:55 hours and the last groups originally scheduled to finish only half an hour earlier, the delay may now see players on the course till late evening.

Delays are disturbing not only to the organizers but also to the players, who then have to struggle with maintaining the rhythm which they develop through previous play days.

The delay in tee-off due to unsavoury weather on the third day of the tournament made golfers restless; some began to kill time with long and easy breakfasts while few others invented waiting games as per their own fancy. Few chose to practice pitching and putting on the practice greens while few others gathered to curse the weather and joke out on their own plight. Those who pulled out their cell phones to check the radar on their own, eventually found themselves scrolling through their social media. Those who detested the infinite scrolls of social media were found idling on the turf, listening to music with a headphone plugged into the phone, in an attempt to keep themselves destressed.

Suddenly, in the distance, above the tall treetops, brightening began that kept building, and a gloomy sun emerged. In the next few minutes, the foggy haze was dispelled, visibility improved and the golf course revealed itself, in its entirety. Finely cut fairways, checkerboard tees, and tabletop greens that were protected by large yawning sand bunkers. The course emerged as the perfect pitch; a befitting setup to test the world's best players.

A stir near the first tee intensified and after some time the TD signalled approval for starting the game. The Starter on the first tee announced the names of the golfers of the first group and the tee-off began. Even though the tee off was delayed by an hour but because the field was reduced already to half on Saturday, owing to the application of cut, the organizers were expecting to finish the game timely for the day.

At the first tee, the build-up of fans was fast. The crowd began to burgeon with the start of the game and soon every seat at the grandstand was occupied. Early in the morning, it was the major spot of action. Also, some people prefer to wait and warm up a little at the first tee before they set out for their day-long walk following golfers on the course.

The event was big, so even the early bird gallery that gathered around the first tee was thick enough. However, for organizers, the biggest challenge was to manage the crowd that was expected when the tee-off for the local stars begins, particularly for the rookie Joy and the champion Jem who were scheduled to tee off at 11 am as per the draw sheet, of course, the delay added an hour to their tee-off too.

The rush around the first tee peaked when the Starter announced, 'Mr Joy Archer, on the tee...' and huge applause charged the surrounding and also the fledgling amateur; he moved forward, pressed a tee on the ground, placed a ball on it, took a stance with eyes fixed on the ball, he drove the ball straight in the middle of the first fairway, that too without a warm-up practice swing. The show was professional!

Next, the name of Jem was announced and he too repeated an exceptional performance, with grace which was well received by the huge gallery from where applause continued for long, warming the already charged ambience, a little more. The golfing duo walked forward following the fairway, and an attendant with a leaderboard placard followed them displaying scores; Mr Joy: -4, and Jem: -5.

Most of the spectators seated on the grandstand near the first tee stood from their seats and joined the fans who were brimming around the tee, and together they began to walk like a block of people parallel to their favourite stars, the two separated only with a thin rope that existed between them.

Unlike DLGR, CGC was an altogether different beast, without getting hurt, taming it demanded an altogether different approach. Here the hazard was not water, the course hardly had any except on the thirteenth that too a small creek with a culvert. However, here the challenge came from the thick forest and its inhabitants. The animals there were not a threat to the players but they certainly were for their game. A bevy of agile deer who burst into a run is no less than a thunderbolt to a player when he concentrated on a shot that mattered most to him.

The first hole of CGC was lined thickly with Golden Shower on both sides, it was a par 5, 500 yards straight hole with a wide-open fairway. Though the trees on either side of the stretch bore black long pods and looked grey, like the weather on that day but during summers, the same trees cause a colour riot. They bloom profusely with long cascading streams of yellow to the extent that the two sides of the stretch appear painted in bright yellow.

Jem and Joy walked briskly and were quick to reach their golf balls which were almost at the centre of the fairway and only a couple of yards apart. Joy took his second shot and the ball landed short of the green, to a pitching distance. Jem pulled his fairway wood and gave it a lofty drive that carried it precariously over the sand bunker that guarded the left corner of the green, eventually coming to rest on the fringe of the green. Joy pitched his ball onto the green that rolled over the slick green, stopping only after finishing its fifteen feet ride. Both Joy and Jem two-putted to finish the first hole, par.

At CGC, the holes two and three were par 4, hole four par 5, and hole five was par 3. Joy and Jem both played these holes successively for par, therefore even after playing five holes the leaderboard that moved with the group remained static reading the same score for the two with which they originally began with the tee-off to begin their round.

However, it was hole six, a par 4, with a length of 410 yards, where Jem's tee shot got inclined to the right and trickled towards a clump of trees, there at a foot of a tree he took an extra shot which made him finish the hole with a bogey. Joy played the hole for par. So, at the finish of the sixth hole both were equal, the gross score on the leaderboard for both was -4.

On the seventh, eighth and ninth holes, Jem managed to remain consistent in his par making while Joy faltered, bogeying the last two holes of front nine one after the other, and thus trailing behind the defending champion. By the finish of the front nine, the aggregate scores for the two popular players on the course were, Joy: -2, Jem: -4.

Unfortunately, the trail of bogeys continued for Joy even in the back nine as he continued to crumble even on the tenth and eleventh holes too, his gross score by the end of the par 5, eleventh was Even. However the waver was for most players on the course, even Jem failed to negotiate the wind and bogeyed the eleventh hole. So finally, the scoreboard at the finish of 480 yards, the eleventh hole were, Joy: E, Jem: -3.

The morning breeze that swept the fog had grown wild by the late afternoon. Judging distances was a challenge, it became difficult for most players to land their golf balls on the fairway. The wind speed deceived their estimation, preventing them from landing on the spot of their choice. They struggled to hold their golf balls on the greens and their scores in minus on the leaderboard. At this point in time, the main leaderboard near the 18th tee had only one single numeral in red, and that was of Jem: -3.

However, by the end of the day, the wind speeds subsided and some birdies began to fly in. As the players succeeded in bagging birdies on the greens and the scores swung back to the colour red. Scorecards of Joy and Jem too registered birdies in the last few holes of the back nine. Joy finished the remaining seven holes with 4 birdies and 3 pars, while Jem bagged 3 birdies and managed 3pars, but he was bogged down at the eighteenth with a bogey. So, at the end of the day their gross scores were, Joy: -4; Jem: -5.

This was the same aggregate score they started their Saturday round, so literally in terms of scores they haven't moved even by a single digit count, in spite of all the day-long struggle in the game, anyway that is what we call golf!

Although on the leaderboard, the scores for the two stars of the tournament remained static on Saturday, still the third day in a golf tournament is generally considered a moving day in a golf event parlance. The cliche' is often used by TV commentators and news reporters but Jem and Joy knew that all days in golf are the same; a new day!

Joy and Jem began their Saturday with a score of -4 and -5 and by the end of the day, it was the same. However, during the day the leaderboard witnessed a fair share of movement around the duo. On the board, names and positions of players kept ascending and descending one over the other and by evening a significant shuffling had occurred on the leaderboard.

On the leaderboard, in relation to the position of Jem and Joy, there were three players above them on Saturday morning, but by the end of the day there were only two above them. Also, the previous three players who were there initially, slipped below them and two new players ascended above them from down the list.

Therefore, with regard to players a moving day may be a mere myth, a mental perception in golf, but in the context of leaderboard and the movement of players positions, it apparently holds veracity.

Sunday

Sunday morning was no different than that of Saturday, it was all fog and no Sun. The tournament was delayed already by an hour from the scheduled tee-off time. The visibility in the course was still poor, it was hard to distinguish turf and trees in distance. An additional delay of thirty more minutes was announced that spiked a restlessness amongst the event organizers, and the players equally. It was certain that if the fog build-up does not diffuse soon, and the weather delay is extended a third time even by a few more minutes, everybody involved in the tournament would find themselves in severe inconvenience.

However, after some time the grey sky slowly began to whiten. The brightness intensified further and high above the forest tree line, behind the curtain of clouds, finally, a feeble Sun was seen, struggling to emerge slowly. Although visibility continued to improve thereafter with every passing minute, the fog apparently was not willing to lose the fight easily to the Sun that Sunday.

Even so, as light always wins over darkness, eventually the sun emerged victorious tearing the layers of smoky fog, the smog with which the capital grapples all through the winters each year.

In most golf tournaments, Sundays are mostly melodramatic for one or the other reason but at CGC even Saturday was not free from criticism when winds got violent during the latter half of the round on Saturday, and led several golfers to falter. It made a few players to blame the tough pin positions on the greens, though in tongue-tied tones but the press which is known to pick up such issues quickly spun it into a controversy. The press took the liberty to air the opinions a little loudly.

But such criticism seemed not to have worked on the Tournament Director, because the pin positions on Sunday appeared even tougher as was obvious on the nearby eighteenth green.

The TD knows better how to bring the best out of each player, and the best player from the field for crowning him as a champion. The course is same for each player irrespective of the set-up, easy or hard, also, the fundamental principle of the game is 'play the ball as it lies, and play the course as you find', champions do not complain, nor do they find faults with the field, they play their best games in all situations.

The game is governed by its rules and not by the players' or press choices. The TD sets up the course that befits the tournament scale, and he conducts it in all fairness following the rules, for he himself is not beyond the purview of the rules of the game.

In this ultimate game of emotions, skills and strategy are necessary and do have their merit, but it primarily is a test of spirits. The greatest moments of thrills in the sport have always been witnessed by the world when the game and a player begin to test each other, with equal stubbornness. The show gets interesting when the game throws a player into the claws of ruthless circumstances to get him crushed, but an ordinary player refuses to give up. In moments of such extreme tests, neither skills nor strategy seems to work, it is the indomitable spirit of the player that helps him rise to the occasion. An ordinary player, with an extraordinary spirit, often emerges as a true champion of the game.

In golf, to have a charged ambience on Sundays is a given. The Sunday round is a deciding one, and it is natural to witness both players and fans high on emotions. Players get anxious thinking about their play, and fans are enthusiastic about their players. However, in the game, those who remain indifferent to the rising commotion around, and could contain their emotions have better chances of success. Those who could continue their pursuit in absolute calm without being carried away by the thoughts of the eventual outcome have the highest possibility of emerging as a champion in the game.

The long delay on Sunday, however, added to the stress of the already stressed players. Though the players who had their scheduled tee-off times later in the day were still better off, as they had the option of adjusting their preparedness and arrival to the club keeping a count of the already announced ninety minutes but for those who had already arrived for their scheduled morning tee-offs, it was tiring. They had been waiting since early morning for the tournament to start. Though they attempted their best to remain cheerful, their faces betrayed the fatigue with which they were suffering even before heading for their day's walk.

A walk without purpose leads nowhere. Therefore, in golf at each hole, the distance between the tee and the hole is performed with a purpose in mind. On the final day of the tournament, a journey of eighteen holes is not merely a walk for a golfer, though it may appear so.

The game of golf that starts from the first tee and ends at the last green appears straightforward as a player is expected only to finish his round based on which he scores. However, the game is a mysterious journey with several subtle aspects to it and so the enlightened ones do not miss on the beauty between the tee and the green. In a golfing journey, it is not about the destination but the journey itself!

For sure, the game is not easy and the terrain through which a player is expected to progress is rough. Further, the journey is an enduring one. No one knows whether it is by chance or by design but certainly, no one escapes the tough and trying times in the game, be it a casual player or a seasoned champion. However, in the game, while treading the terrain of the track some of the seasoned players rise to such elevations of spirits that they begin to excel at cherishing not only the highs but also the lows that they encounter.

During the journey, there may be times when nobody is looking. However, in equity, it is expected from all players to act in all fairness to the field. These are the moments where how one conducts himself matters most.

The credits for impeccable conduct may not always translate into an immediate trophy or a paycheck but possibly the game has its other ways also to appreciate its players. Such players often succeed in leaving their indelible marks on the track even after they are gone. Is it not what we call satisfaction or salvation? Where we rise above the game itself and begin to live in the hearts and minds of the generations to come. Where we become the mascot of the game for the other players too when they are on the same track after us. As a light, we begin to guide them in the darkest hours of their journeys.

To err is human, and mistakes while playing are possible, they are not forbidden either in the game, for there are penalties to take care of such minor aberrations. Also, if one lands in a fix while playing, in some particular situations the player has an option to redeem himself at the cost of incurring penalties. But cheating is taboo in the game, and quitting the game in the middle of a round for no sane reason is a sin, for sure!

If one is really tired of running the race for long, it is alright to look for a break, but to quit is not in good grace. Quitting the game is not expected from the ones who are chosen for the game. In the game every player is equal, and every player is a potential champion. So, when one is blessed with an opportunity to be a part of this divine design, why not put our best that befits our origin and also bring glory to the game and honour to the one who is behind it and reposed his faith by choosing us for his game.

While on his long pursuit, a player always has an option to pause for some time, take a break, relax and reset the self and get back in it with fresh vigour and perspective. A golfer necessarily is not expected to play all tournaments, it is fine to become a silent spectator of the game for some time, observe and contemplate the deeper meanings of the game before getting back into the competition and continuing onwards.

Further, the game is not only about the ongoing competition in the course but off the course too, there is a lot that can be contributed to the game, provided one can look earnestly for his place and purpose in the larger game. We can see many such fighters around us that the game brings to the fore who keep their connect with the game even when time renders them unfit for the severe competition. The fight is not entirely of physical faculties but is of spirits, of all the emotions in the game the spirit to survive in the game is the strongest, and it is equally honoured by the game.

Mr Mark, the young committee member of CGC and the aspiring captain for the club is one such player of indomitable spirit. Once he was a young golfer, full of aspirations, brimming with ambitions but when he met an unfortunate accident a few years ago losing his swing, and his dreams of becoming a successful player on the tour, he didn't give up, he didn't quit. Instead, he chose to look for his place and purpose in the game after all everybody has a role to play, it is all about finding one.

In his newfound role as the custodian of the game, where he served the game by serving on the committee of the club, he was no less content. He was in absolute bliss even among the sea of spectators who gathered around the first tee expecting the arrival of two local heroes of the ongoing competition. As a spectator, standing silently amongst the crowd without being in the limelight, he silently cherished the game that is so dear to him, through young golfers like Jem and Joy.

The grandstand at first tee was already full. Nobody wanted to risk their seats to the continuously building crowd, so the spectators remained sticking to their seats till it was time for Jem and Joy to tee off. The show that began on Sunday with the warmth of the applause at the first tee was now reaching its crescendo as the duo of Jem and Joy was expected at any moment.

Finally, the wait was over, for which the teeming fans of the two golfers and their clubs were anxiously waiting. Jem and Joy arrived and were greeted on the first tee for the final round of the National Open. The two golfers were again reintroduced to the spectators formally with the announcement of their names.

As on Saturday, the two players, an amateur and the professional, both struck their first tee shots with firm confidence and professionalism almost in the same way they did the past day, landing almost in the centre of the fairway. However, Joy lagged Jem by a single stroke with a gross score of -4, compared to -5 of Jem. On Sunday morning as on Saturday the scores on the leaderboard for the two didn't move, but in golf, every day is a new beginning. Every day is a new day, a new play full of possibilities for every player.

Joy birdied while Jem parred the hole and so by the end of the first hole on Sunday, score-wise both an amateur and a professional were on the same plank. The scores for the two were, Mr Joy: -5, and Jem: -5.

Attribute it to their individual effort or the design of the game, today on the final day, at this point they were equal, with equal opportunities for the future, although their scores were different on the first two days of the tournament. However, it was not over yet, as they progress through the day, the choices they would make while playing the remaining holes would eventually decide their final fate.

As they moved carefully trying to gain an edge over the other, and once one had a lead over the other even by a margin, the attempt was to widen it, there was a stiff fight. The par 4, second hole was played par by both, on third, however, Jem shot a birdie and was -6, while Joy stayed at -5 playing it for a par. On fourth, Jem again birdied and the edge got sharper with Jem at -7 and Joy still at -5. However, on the fifth, Jem fumbled making a bogey whereas Joy continued to play for par. At the hole sixth, Jem tried to play safe, but sensing an opportunity Joy grabbed a birdie and again they were equal with a score of -6, each.

On the hole seventh, Jem shot a birdie followed by another one at the eighth while Joy continued to keep his nerves calm and played for par. The lead Jem had now was again of two shots with a score of -8.

Nevertheless, at the ninth hole Joy was able to extract a birdie for himself and improved his score to -7, and Jem shanked his shot that he tried to carry too far and landed in the woods. It was a nightmare for him to get out of the area where the 'god of golf' does not come to rescue, it is a domain of a different deity. He finished the hole with a double-bogey with a gross score of -6.

Therefore, though Jem had the lead of one when they started their morning round, by the end of front nine, the lead reversed. However, both made progress in the front nine, improved their scores and moved up on the leaderboard displaying good and consistent golf.

The procession of the fans following their heroes of the day passed quickly from the ninth green to the tenth tee which was a reasonable walk across the adjoining clubhouse. The tenth hole ended with an eagle for Jem where he hit his shot from off the putting green but never needed to putt it as it rolled straight into the hole. However, Joy played it for par. The gross scores for Joy and Jem on the leaderboard were now, -7, and -8, respectively.

Jem played the hole eleventh for a par but Joy fumbled again and bogeyed the hole. There was a continuous shower of birdies from Jem for the next two holes, hole twelfth and thirteenth giving him an impressive lead of four strokes with an overall score of -10. Joy had no option but to remain content with his pars and with a score of -6. The trying time has begun for Joy, the pressure was enough to crumble any ordinary player but he kept carrying himself patiently, perhaps believing his own strategy, self, and maybe the gods of golf!

When the lead widened continuously, and few holes only were left to be played, there was rising anxiety amongst the members of the DLGR. Their hopes of seeing their home club hero as the champion was slowly thinning out. Some began to console the fellow members by suggesting that it is alright, after all, he is just an amateur and is giving a good fight to the hardened professionals to whom the tournament actually belongs.

Though the fans attempted to console themselves with all kinds of excuses but in a corner of their heart, they still wished for a miracle. Interestingly, this secret wish was not only in the hearts of DLGR members but impressed with the fight given by a rookie, even members of the CGC fancied to see him succeed in the game.

Prayers are heard sometimes in the game, probably, and certainly if they are well-meaning and made earnestly. Fourteenth, fifteenth and sixteenth were played in a ziffy and Joy quickly bagged three birdies in succession, while Jem had a shock of settling for par, though at the end of the sixteenth hole he still led by a shot. The leaderboard rolled with scores transforming quickly, now for Joy, it was -9 and for Jem, -10.

Also at the end of this hole, they were now the overall leaders in the field, this certainly was news of pleasure for the fans but what emotion it aroused in the hearts of the two players, only they knew. On the leaderboard, all others have slipped down making it a one-to-one fight between the two for the next two holes.

The hole seventeenth, a short par 3 was played par and interestingly, both missed the much-needed birdie. Eventually, it was long, par 5, the eighteenth hole where the game was about to unfold its real champion. With every shot, the huge crowd held their hearts, and also breaths to ensure a pin-drop silence when the shots were performed, they avoided even a slightest distraction to the players in their game. Finally, Jem missed a birdie again and picked his ball for par from the finishing hole of the game. Now, the final putt for Joy was no more a mere putt, anymore.

On the eighteenth green, his ball lay some 20 feet from the hole. Sinking such a putt is not impossible but neither is it a cake walk for any golfer; in such moments every player looks for a little divine intervention and kindness from the game itself. Missing the putt meant not only the loss of the game for him but also his life's love. However making this difficult putt doesn't make him win this game either, however, it would make him even with his opponent. Which would ensure a 'play-off' between the two players to decide the final champion.

It was obvious that thousands of fans uttered their prayers within their hearts, the course was observing a pin-drop silence. The uncommon silence, an absolute trance, no sound at all. Joy, focused himself completely on the golf ball, with his putter hovering over the ball, swung back gently in a rhythm and returned to kiss the white beauty on the green, it rolled straight, and then at the contour, curved gracefully, finally it was home, in the hole!

The course ruptured with cheers, joy, and emotions, all in a single burst. The prayers from the fans were probably loud enough to be missed by the god of golf. The gross scores that froze on the leaderboard for the two leaders of the tournament were, Joy: -10, and Jem: -10.

Play Off

The long twenty-foot putt that was sunk on the eighteenth green resulted in a tie between Joy and Jem. Ties in the game could be settled in multiple ways, but 'sudden death playoff' as they call it, is one of the most common and straightforward ways. In this, two players play extra holes again and again until one player outlives the other by playing better. Under extreme stress of playoff, the player who can hold longer in the field emerges as a winner and is consequently crowned champion of a tournament.

At CGC, by the time final round ended in a tie between Joy and Jem, the setting sun was hanging on the horizon, feeble and faint. It was late; the dusk had begun to fall. The forest was already fuzzy, and it seemed as if the evening fog waited on the fringes of fairways just for the game to culminate before caving in, all over the course, again.

The TD was desperate to get the tournament concluded before dark, at the earliest to avoid any controversy on its culmination. Therefore, a 545-yard-long distance of the hole was performed quickly by two golf carts of Rules Officials, and with them, the two players were back on the 18th tee.

Jem stood on the 18th tee again, but he found himself a little restless. He tried focusing on the white golf ball that rested on a raised tee but in that he saw two young faces; one of his sister's, Jas and the other of Joy, her happiness! His thoughts, like a nimble butterfly, flitted from one face to the other.

The game is known for its notoriety to test its players in all odd ways. The test certainly is toughest when one has to fight his closest relations for the sake of the game and when the opponent is none other than someone dear to one's heart, it is particularly painful.

Jem and Joy were friends, more so Jem realized that his long career was replete with wins. One more win would merely be a one more triumph to his credit whereas a win for Joy in the tournament would matter a lot not only to him but also to his sister, whose happiness was pinned to the outcome of the ongoing game.

In the game at times, we witness a player refusing to bend, and with his sheer fight he even foils the design of destiny but some other times surviving the onslaught is tough. What of ordinary players, even the hardened players get crushed in the grindstones of emotions; dilemmas, conflicts, ethics, and morality. The most virtuous of the players who succeed through everything else, often fall for the emotions, especially when the happiness of a loved one is at stake.

Anyway, the keepers of the game are in plenty but the game is only one, and the game should go on! This idea in the sport is held in all earnestness because the Bravehearts of this game come from the very grind of the game. They assert their claim on the trophy irrespective of the costs involved which makes them its worthy claimant.

Whether it is the game or its players, important? It may be hard to say. However, at the altar of time as often as not the emotions of players mostly get mercilessly sacrificed, and the game often takes precedence.

Jem reined in his emotions back. He held back the thoughts that came rushing to him, prompting him to concede to the temptations of making an emotional choice motivated by his personal and family happiness. Though nobody would ever be able to detect what went on within him and the world would never blame him for his own defeat in the competition, he was aware that it would be a dent on the spirit of the game.

He knew it would not be a mere mistake but to let it happen would be a sin. This burden of not playing in the spirit of the game would linger on his soul for the rest of his life. Therefore, resisting vehemently the thoughts of letting his adversary win by compromising his own play, he recollected himself and prepared for his best play again, whatever it takes him through.

From the 18th tee, Jem played a fine tee shot again, and the ball came zooming in towards the hole where the crowd was high on energy. The ball landed perfectly for the next shot right in the middle of the fairway. Joy's drive however took a little sway to a left and landed off the centre but still in the fairway, and in a fairly decent lie.

The two walked to their golf balls where a huge crowd was in waiting to see their next shot from close. Jem's second shot landed on the right side of a bunker which guarded the eighteenth green. A loud roar of applause from the distance near the green assured the player that the ball was safe from the sand escaping the beach.

When it was Joy's turn, he avoided the sand bunker by making perfectly clean shot with an impressive long carry, however, to everyone surprise after touching the turf his ball rolled into the bushes on the right of the fairway.

For a few moments the spectators were stunned to witness such a weird bounce of a well-played ball. They wondered how a perfect shot that landed so beautifully on the fairway could take such an ugly bounce into the bushes.

The cameras zoomed in anticipation, probing for an embedded stone in the turf but in vain. However, when Joy passed through the spot from where his ball deflected in the deathly direction, he saw a glistening metal marker. A golf ball-marker that might have slipped off unknowingly from a hat-clip of some player while in the field.

It was a 'rub of the green', though this time it was the most devastating one for Joy. Still, he remained unruffled, calm; without any wrinkle of resentment on his face. At such a grim moment, like a champion he bent gracefully, picked the metal coin, and slipped it in his pocket maybe to spare a similar ordeal to some other golfer. Though, keeping it just as memorabilia of a biggest deceit of chance too was justified at that moment.

At this ruthless injustice of chance to a young golfer the crowd broke into commotion, they felt pity at his plight. But rules are rules, and everyone was helpless in the situation. The spirit of the fans sank suddenly, and all were silent then. The lull pervaded not only amongst the lobby of Joy's own home club but the gloom got even into the pavilion of CGC.

At such an intense show of the sport, that too by a young player the thought of belonging to different clubs thinned out amongst the spectators. The fans seemed to have been supporting the spirit of the game, cheering for the good game rather than who the player was and from where he came.

Joy displayed such a fine golf and a gentlemanly demeanour that at the spur of the moment even the members of CGC were seen rooting for him. Probably in their hearts, they too had begun to wish for the victory of the young rookie.

When his golf ball bounced into the bushes, everybody got disturbed including the members of CGC. Even they did not expect him to lose this way when he had come so far already.

Unfortunately, now the tournament was considered almost over, as the next stroke from behind the bushes was almost an impossible feat to accomplish. A penalty drop appeared the only option for Joy, which would practically make it impossible for him to win the Play Off hole from Jem, who was just a pitch shot away from the green.

By now, the dusk had fallen and the floodlights on the eighteenth green were lit up, so putting was not an issue. But, though in present scenario practically it seemed an almost impossible proposition, had there been a tie again in the playoff round, there would have been no other way but to defer a further playoff to the next day because the fog had already caved in from all sides in the course.

Anyhow, seeking his ball Joy entered the thick bushes in a least intrusive manner. It was already hazy inside; the surroundings were dull but in the little light that filtered in through the bushes, his golf ball, glistening white, was visible to him.

Joy stood some seventy yards from the pin and his ball lay on a pile of forest litter. He took his stance carefully and realized that in between the ball and the pin there were two thin trees, but there also existed an opportunity; about a foot gap across the two slender stems. He eyed the target through the narrow gap between two branches, the flag was in direct vision.

Large crowds loomed outside the bushes but Joy was all alone in the woody cavern to perform a toughest stroke of the game, and possibly of his life. He stretched his club back as if in preparation to assess the available swing, the pin was not too far so a full swing was anyway not needed. However, for sure the shot demanded an exceptional focus and a precision of a dead shot to shoot a ball through a narrow crack to reach the green.

The ball was clearly unplayable in all other directions except towards the pin flag, that too through a tiny breach which existed between the two tree branches.

Even if such a shot was crossing the mind of Joy, to shoot a golf ball with a club having an accuracy of a gun was an almost impossible feat to accomplish. The player, however, seemed to have decided. He steadied his stance, arced his club for about a quarter swing, and hit a shot that appeared unreal for few moments; the spectators were awestruck.

There was a clean contact of the club and the ball in dark, and suddenly a ball popped out from the bushes kissing cleanly the fringe of the green and rolling some 10 yards straight, burying itself quickly into the hole for an eagle at the 18th.

The cheer in response was loud enough to be heard beyond the boundaries of the course. The game was turned by the skill of the player. Or by a sheer luck? No one knew for sure; the world always remains divided on merits of luck and skills in the game.

No one ever had an eye and the wisdom to discern what plays behind a player in such raw situations that renders unrealistic results in a game. However, yet again a player proved that emerging victorious even in the most impossible of situations is all about playing one's best game with trust and self-belief.

A player may not know the result but he certainly chooses a stroke that he makes. Therefore, for every stroke that a player makes he ought to own it, even if it is more of luck and less of, he himself, or the other way round.

Unwinding himself from the bushes, Joy emerged. Walking towards the green he waved to the highly cheerful crowd, and picked his ball from the hole. Jem then pitched his ball on the green and putted to finish the par 5 hole with a birdie, but still losing the playoff and the tournament. The scores for the play-off hole were, Joy: 3, Jem: 4.

Fans and friends of Joy were just on the verge of the green 18th, ready to rush towards Joy. They, however, waited for him to have a final handshake with his playing partner Jem to formally finish the round. Jem who was happy to lose for the first time in his life proceeded to Joy for a handshake, but surprisingly, Joy appeared to have refrained. Instead, he called for a Rules Official and spoke something to him.

The rules official quickly communicated with the TD on the radio. The cameraman who shot the last stroke of Joy on the field was called; the attending rules official at the eighteenth green tried to see the shot with wide-open eyes on the display screen of the camera but nothing unusual appeared to him. The feed sent from the field camera was the only record of the final shot of Joy, and it flashed time and again on the large digital screen, nothing unusual was apparent either on that too. He talked to a referee again, on his request who was busy reviewing the final stroke in slow-mo in the TV room.

Nobody had any clue what was happening, people were dying to see Joy lift the trophy and celebrate the phenomenal success of a champion of the game. However, something was going on, only the player and the referees knew about it. The reviewing referee was not able to decide and take a final call on the situation; before being hit, whether the ball moved or not!

Finally, Hari, the TD and the Chief Referee, who was responsible for conducting the game in all fairness, reached the TV room. He observed the visuals again in slow motion and announced his ruling, a 2-stroke penalty, and thus the result; a final verdict!

Though, he was highly moved by the honesty with which Joy upheld the spirit of the game but as per his observation, the ball moved, before being struck by his club; though minutely. And the mistake was attributed to the player.

In golf, even a TD cannot wave a penalty for a player's action and a consequent breach of a rule in the game. After all, he is the custodian of the rules and the game. Every player in the field is the responsibility of the TD, and he is duty-bound to act in fairness to the field, without any attachment, bias, or prejudice.

In the game, no action can go without a result, and no one escapes the results of his acts. Even the one who runs the game is bound by the rules of the game.

There was a severe silence of monotony for some time. Then slowly the crowd and the media began with all the exuberant praises and adorations for the young amateur who played like a professional.

Though he lost the competition, he won a tremendous honour in the hearts of the golfing fans. He eventually played for the spirit of the game and took its flag another notch up, and higher. After application of the 2-stroke penalty to Joy's score, the adjusted scores finally for the Play Off were, Mr Joy: 5; Jem: 4. With this sudden flip of scores, Joy lost the Play Off and consequently the Tournament to Jem.

Eventually, as fans overcame the shock and saw Joy walking off the 18th green after a handshake with his playing partner, the champion, fans burst into cheers and rushed towards the 18th green. The major rush of golf fans however was after Joy rather than the champion of the tournament.

Joy was the new mascot of the game, a new star that had suddenly shone so gloriously in the sporting firmament of the world that everybody across the clubs and courses talked about him, and his honesty. The press and media were busy spilling ink, filling scrolls of papers with headlines about the stories of a young rookie amateur who lost the trophy but won hearts of millions of seekers of the game.

Bubbles, however, wrote the following story for her news network:

'... playoff between an amateur, Joy and a professional player, Jem ended with a dramatic flip of victory from Joy to Jem by 1-stroke. On a detailed review of a video that was available of the last shot of playoff, the TD of the tournament decided that the ball moved. He ruled that the ball was played from a ''wrong place'' and so attracted a 2-stroke penalty to the score of finished final hole. It was noted that the ball lay on a tip of a wood log that was buried beneath the litter and soil. The player stepped on the other end of the buried wood branch while taking a stance for his shot, and caused the ball to move by a fraction. In dim light it might have escaped Joy's eye, but not his conscience. Consequently, realizing his mistake, like a professional player he requested the tournament committee to review and rule his final shot which otherwise would have gone unnoticed, for sure.

'The playoff at CGC was a sudden death to several emotions of the fans who got attached to the player and his play, more than the game. The player, however, had played it without any attachment, without worrying about its outcome, in the spirit of the game!'

Epilogue: The Result and Reward

The elections for the Captain and the Club Committee of CGC were near, the dates were already announced by the Secretariat and Open House meeting and the elections on the same date were due in two weeks. The different lobbies in the club were already on their work of canvassing for their candidates. Secret alliances, private meetings and fun parties at the farmhouses of the contesting members for the club committee elections had already begun in the capital, to seek their vote and support.

However, the present president of the club, Mr Billy had a better pretext of throwing a public party and thereby wooing the voting members at large, everybody from the club was invited to the 'felicitation party' organized to honour the recent club champion of the National Open, Jem, his son. The party was aimed to lobby the votes for his younger brother, Mr Mark, the captain candidate from the Greens' family of the club.

It was a party thrown by the CGC President primarily for his own club members. Some of the top players of the DLGR including Joy were invited as special guests, the party was to felicitate golfing heroes of the capital who played great golf during the past week.

In the sprawling lawns of the CGC, a nice open bar was laid for the guests, and soft music played. The evening was getting young as more and more guests kept joining. Joy, like a gentlemen celebrity, arrived with his few golfer friends and was immediately honoured by the crowd as he walked through, with cheerful applause and admiration.

Joy, however, before taking a seat walked straight to Mr Stuart, and handed over an envelope to him. The secretary opened the envelope and as he took a quick look at the content, his face brightened and he thanked Joy with a smiling face. He then quickly rushed to the tables where Mr Billy was sitting with a group of his friends and family.

He ducked a little, to reach his ear, from a side, and softly said, 'We have received the papers.'

'Which papers?', questioned the president.

'The papers of the 18th green, land transfer papers signed by Mr Bobby', answered the secretary.

With this, the matter of the 18th green land dispute was resolved forever.

Billy thought of announcing this important news to the gathered club members and thereby gain on the support for his brother. It certainly was a key canvassing instrument in his hand at the moment but he saw the captain already on the dais addressing the members, so he waited for him to finish.

On the dais, the captain announced that he has received a letter from Hari, the Tournament Director of the recently held event of National Open on behalf of the tour and he wanted to share it with the patrons of the club, and the members.

The letter was all thanks and gratitude to the club for being a kind host and presenting the course in immaculate conditions, etc. but the lines that moved everybody were, '...my congratulations to the champion and the star player of your club, Jem. However, I feel proud to witness two champions during the event at your course, one the champion of the competition and the other, the champion of the game!' Hearing these lines there was long and continued applause and cheers for the two champions in whose honour the party was hosted.

On hearing this, Billy could not hide the emotional turmoil that began within him. Sensing the turbulence on his brother's face, Bubbles, who was at the same table, asked him, 'Billy, don't you feel that the champion of the game is greater than the champion of any golf event?'

'Yes, I do believe, said Billy.

'If you do believe then you too have a promise to keep,' said Bubbles assertively.

Joy, undisputedly emerged as the true champion of the game, it was obvious to everybody, and Billy too, in his heart could not avoid acknowledging it. There was some sort of inner churning going in his head and as the captain descended the dais, Billy rose from his seat and walked to the podium looking for a mic. He drew the attention of the audience and said that he too has some good news to share with his larger family, the members of the club.

He, then announced, 'I am proud to have a player like Joy amongst us all these years, who learned his game on this very turf which we all cherish, although now he has his own course just next to us. I am highly proud to see him emerge as the greatest champion of the game during the recent event. I, therefore, am bound to keep my word. I hereby announce the engagement of my daughter, Jas with the greatest champion of the game!'

The party burst into cheers. Jas could not contain her emotions and hugged her aunt seated next to her, but Joy, like always carried himself gracefully, with a restrained smile, shaking hands with his friends and colleagues.

As the crescendo of the crowd's cheers passed a little, he further added, 'I have one more very important piece of news to share with the members of the club, the 18th green land dispute with my friend Bobby is settled, the secretariat has received the land transfer papers from him recently.'

The cheers and uproar of celebrations again reverberated loudly. Finally, the long-pending matters between the two clubs came to a resolution. The members were happy to see that the dispute that started during the captaincy of Billy, also reached its resolution during his own presidency. The party and celebrations continued.

Joy, in his heart silently thanked Hari and remembered what he said to him after declaring his decision on the rule issue when he later met him in private. After announcing his verdict on the final day, the TD had told him in private that he felt pity for him but he was helpless as he himself was bound by the rules. However, he appreciated his honesty and assured him that in the long run he would certainly be rewarded by the 'gods of golf' for his exemplary conduct in the game.

The letter from Hari, came as the greatest reward for him today. His belief in himself and in the game eventually rendered him with the greatest happiness of his life.

We are always clueless about the future but sometimes things happen as we wish them. When our wishes are realized we wonder, how things happen as we dreamt of them happening. When wishes come true, we are left thinking about whether it was our prayers, our actions or sheer emotions behind all this. Probably it is all of this.

If the game is played without worrying about its outcome, it is full of possibilities. Though the results of the game are anyway beyond the control of players, the game, however, rewards its true players for sure. The players who play it in the spirit of the game, eventually are rewarded, in all unexpected ways!